ALSO BY RICHARD PAUL EVANS

RICHARD PAUL EVANS

The Broken Road

SIMON & SCHUSTER

New York   London   Toronto   Sydney   New Delhi

Simon & Schuster
1230 Avenue of the Americas
New York, NY 10020

Copyright © 2017 by Richard Paul Evans

All rights reserved, including the right to reproduce this book or portions thereof in any form whatsoever. For information, address Simon & Schuster Subsidiary Rights Department, 1230 Avenue of the Americas, New York, NY 10020.

First Simon & Schuster hardcover edition May 2017

SIMON & SCHUSTER and colophon are registered trademarks of Simon & Schuster, Inc.

For information about special discounts for bulk purchases, please contact Simon & Schuster Special Sales at 1-866-506-1949 or business@simonandschuster.com.

The Simon & Schuster Speakers Bureau can bring authors to your live event. For more information or to book an event, contact the Simon & Schuster Speakers Bureau at 1-866-248-3049 or visit our website at www.simonspeakers.com.

Interior design by Joy O'Meara

Manufactured in the United States of America

1   3   5   7   9   10   8   6   4   2

Library of Congress Cataloging-in-Publication Data is available.

ISBN 978-1-5011-1164-8
ISBN 978-1-5011-1178-5 (ebook)

To Jonathan Karp

Prologue

When I began writing this story, I thought I had some idea of what it was about. I was wrong. In my life of writing I've discovered that there are times when a story, like architecture, is carefully designed, erected, and furnished. Then there are tales that take their own way, and I find myself being dragged along after them like a white-knuckled water skier behind a speedboat.

This tale is the latter. My plan was to write about the changing, perhaps fading, of the American identity. The perfect metaphor of this change was a road, a dying road with many names—the Will Rogers Highway, Main Street America, the Mother Road—the infamous Route 66.

That's what I *thought* I was writing about. But the road I followed took me somewhere else. Or, more correctly, to *someone* else. It was near the end of my journey that I met a dead man.

⋅━◉━⋅

Back to Route 66. I wouldn't be the first writer to take on the legendary highway. Hundreds, maybe thousands of articles have been written about Route 66, and even some greats, like Steinbeck and Kerouac, have contributed to the collection.

It has also been celebrated in film and song. The eponymous television series, *Route 66*, starred some of the biggest actors of all time, including Burt Reynolds, William Shatner, Tuesday Weld, James Caan, Robert Redford, and Ron Howard.

In music, the 1946 Bobby Troup song "Get Your Kicks on Route 66" has been performed by myriad musicians including Nat King Cole, the Rolling Stones, and Depeche Mode.

In its heyday, Route 66 was far more than asphalt. It was a path that Americans trekked as pioneers to a new world of opportunity, imaginary or otherwise. It was the American dream.

⋅━◉━⋅

I began my journey on a Friday afternoon in early fall. I was living in Chicago at the time, which is the beginning of the route.

I knew from my research that the road was about 2,500 miles, give or take a few towns, so when I left my home that day, my plan was to drive 250 miles a day, completing the journey in about ten days. What I didn't know then was that Route 66 doesn't surrender itself that easily; rather, it must be hunted down, sometimes with the tenacity of a detective. There are two reasons for this.

First, there's not just one Route 66. During its active years, parts of the road changed multiple times.

Second, sections of the original highway now lie beneath new roads, homes, and developments. There are places where metropolises, like Chicago, St. Louis, and Oklahoma City, have grown up around the highway with hundreds of new roads fragmenting the route into pieces like a mosaic. Sometimes it gets confusing. Sometimes downright ridiculous. In Albuquerque, New Mexico, the route actually crosses itself and you can stand on the corner of Route 66 and Route 66.

Even where the road hasn't faced urban development, there are remote, forsaken places no longer traveled where the road has died and been reclaimed by nature, with vegetation growing up through its deteriorating, cracked asphalt.

Route 66 runs through eight states—Illinois, Missouri, Kansas, Oklahoma, Texas, New Mexico, Arizona, and California—and each of these states regards (or disregards) the route in its own way. Varying colors of signs mark the path—blue, brown, black, and white—while in some places, weary of the constant road sign stealing by nostalgic collectors, states have simply painted the Route 66 shield onto the asphalt.

It took me two weeks to reach Needles, a city on the eastern border of California on the edge of the Mojave

Desert—four days longer than I thought my entire journey would take me. By then I was no longer bothered by the difficulty of the way. I felt a fondness for the road, like a wildlife photographer tracking the last of a dying species. But I also knew that I was near the end of my journey and I still hadn't found my story.

Needles was the first California town that the Okies—fleeing the famine of the Dust Bowl to the supposed paradise of California—encountered. This is where Carty's Camp, from John Steinbeck's *The Grapes of Wrath*, was located.

Sitting on the western edge of the Mojave Desert, Needles, like its northwestern cousin Death Valley, is the kind of place that sets national temperature records. There are days the temperature reaches 130-plus degrees.

I suppose that's why I noticed *him*—the man who was to become my story. The first time I saw him he was sitting alone at a booth in the famous Wagon Wheel Restaurant. Judging by the large, dusty pack next to him, it appeared that he was hiking through this hell. He was dark featured, though I couldn't discern his ethnicity. He was deeply tanned and unshaven, disheveled but handsome in spite of it. Or maybe because of it.

His clothes were wet with sweat, with myriad salt lines staining his shirt, not only under his arms but across his chest and trim stomach as well. The temperature that day was 119 degrees, hot enough to tax the air conditioner of my rental car. Out of curiosity, I had rolled down my window just outside of Needles. It felt like I was driving through a convection oven. I couldn't imagine walking through it carrying a pack. Actually, carrying anything besides water.

⤑═◉═⤐

The Wagon Wheel Restaurant had the façade of an old-time western building. Inside, past a gift shop stocked with Route 66 paraphernalia (signs, clocks, coasters, pencils, etc.), was a large dining room lit by ceiling lights made of metal wagon wheels with amber glass sconces.

My server, a blond woman with thick, dark mascara who was wearing a pink Wagon Wheel T-shirt, left me at a booth beneath a poster of Marilyn Monroe—the famous flying skirt picture from *The Seven Year Itch*.

The restaurant was nearly vacant, and besides my waitress (and Miss Monroe), there was only the hiker, who was carefully wiping his table with an antiseptic wipe. Considering his sweat and dust-crusted attire, he didn't look the part of a germophobe.

When my waitress returned, I ordered lemonade, chicken-fried steak, and a cup of navy bean and ham soup, then picked up my notepad and began recording my surroundings.

My waitress brought me the lemonade and returned to the kitchen. I furtively glanced back over at the man. He had finished wiping down his table and had arranged his silverware symmetrically. He was reading a book.

Everything about this man looked out of place. There was a properness to how he held himself that didn't quite seem congruent with his dress or circumstance. But there was something else that caught my attention: he looked familiar.

He suddenly looked up from his book, and we shared eye contact. He tipped his head. I felt a little embarrassed being caught looking at him.

"Hot enough for you?" I asked.

"Yes, sir." He returned to his book.

I returned a few text messages while I finished my lemonade. When my waitress came out with a refill, I asked, "Where's your washroom?"

"It's right over there," she said, pointing to the far back corner of the room.

When I returned to my booth, the man had a plate of food in front of him—a T-bone steak, mashed potatoes, and gravy. He suddenly looked up at me and asked, "Are you from Chicago?"

I looked at him with surprise. His voice and articulation were smoother than I expected. "How did you guess?"

"You asked for the *washroom*. That, and your accent. I'd guess the upper east side."

"I'm from Lakeshore East," I said. "You're from Chicago?"

"Yes, sir."

"What part?"

"Oak Park."

His answer surprised me. Like everything else about him, even his hometown seemed incongruent. Oak Park was an upscale suburban village to the west of Chicago. I always thought there must be something special in the water in Oak Park, because it had spawned more than its share of world shakers—the famous and infamous. Writers Ernest Hemingway and Edgar Rice Burroughs, architect Frank Lloyd Wright, and in business, Ray Kroc, the founder of McDonald's; Richard Sears, of Sears, Roebuck & Company; even James Dewar, the inventor of the Twinkie.

There were also TV and radio personalities including Betty White, Paul Harvey, Bob Newhart, Hannah Storm, and Peter Sagal. On the infamous side, there were crime bosses Joseph Aiuppa and Sam Giancana.

"Nice part of town," I said. When he didn't comment I added, "You're a long way from Oak Park."

A curious smile crossed his lips, but all he said was, "*Farther* than you can imagine."

"You'd have to be crazy to be walking in this heat," I said.

He took a sip of his water, then said, "They don't let me set the thermostat."

"Do people stop to give you rides?"

He shook his head. "I'm not looking for rides. Water, sometimes, but not rides."

"It seems kind of dangerous."

"Life *is* dangerous."

Again, he seemed strangely familiar. "Where did you start walking?"

"The beginning," he said.

"The beginning of what?"

"Route 66."

"You walked the whole way from Chicago?"

"Started on Jackson Street, across from the Bean."

"The Bean" referred to the Cloud Gate sculpture at Millennium Park in Downtown Chicago. It was the same place I'd begun. "You walked the entire way?"

"Yes, sir."

"Why?"

"Now that's a question," he said, sidestepping mine. "What about you? What brings you to Needles?"

"I'm writing a book about Route 66. I'm a novelist."

"What's your story about?"

"I thought it was a nostalgia piece about the changing of America—sort of a *Travels with Charley* meets Garrison Keillor. But now I'm not sure where it's going." I looked at him, still curious. "What's your story? What makes a man walk twenty-five hundred miles?"

"What do you think would make a man walk twenty-five hundred miles?"

I hesitated with my answer. "Honestly, my first thought was that maybe you were a little *off*."

He laughed. "You wouldn't be the first to think that."

"But since you're not, I'd guess you're running from something."

"You're getting warmer," he said. "What's your name?"

"Richard," I said.

"Richard what?"

"My writing name is Richard Paul Evans."

"I've heard of you. You write Christmas books."

"Some of them are," I said. "My first book was."

"What's your genre?"

"The publishing world has had trouble with that. I've

found my books shelved in literature, inspirational, romance, religious . . ." I trailed off. "What's your name?"

"Charles." He hesitated a moment, then said, "Charles James."

"You share a famous name."

"Should I know this person?"

"I hope not," I said.

"Why is that?"

"He was a huckster. He made millions selling get-rich-quick scams to the gullible. He was killed in that O'Hare plane crash last year. Flight 227." I suddenly remembered where the article had said he was from. "James also lived in Oak Park. You must have known him."

Without flinching he said, "I thought I did."

For a moment we just looked at each other. Then, through his sunburned skin, beard, and long hair, I suddenly recognized who I was talking to. I think he must have realized that I'd figured it out, because his mouth rose in a slight grin. "Yes?"

"You're supposed to be dead," I said.

"Charles James is."

I just gazed at him for a long moment. "Tell me your story."

"What makes you think I'd want to share it?" He took another drink and abruptly went back to his meal as if he were done talking to me.

I watched him for a minute, then said, "I think you do."

"Why would you say that?"

"Because you told me your full name."

He looked back up, and his grin reappeared. "I have

thought about it. In fact, I've started to write my story. Writing isn't new to me. I've published three books. One of them was a *New York Times* bestseller for a couple of weeks."

"I remember that. Something like *Making the Millionaire*."

"*Waking Your Inner Millionaire*," he corrected.

"Right," I said. "So you're a writer like me."

"Not like you," he said. "There's a big difference between us. I write nonfiction, you write fiction. I write truths that tell lies. You write lies that tell truths."

I smiled. "You started writing your book?"

"Twice. But it wasn't right. I think I'm too close to the acorns to see the forest. Does that make sense?"

"Complete sense."

"It takes a certain . . . sensitivity to write romance. And on the deepest level, my story is a romance. I didn't realize that when I started, but I do now."

"There's a broken heart behind most journeys," I said. "From Beowulf to Ulysses."

He looked at me for a moment and said, "So you think you're the kind of writer who could write my story?"

"Maybe. If I'm not, we'd know soon enough."

He shook his head. "Like I said, I've thought a lot about this. *If* I gave it to you, it would come with conditions. You won't like them."

"Try me."

"All right. First, no one is to see the book or even know that I'm still alive until I tell you. It could be a month; it could be a decade. The story's not over yet, and I'm still not sure how it ends. If anyone finds out, it could ruin everything."

"Fair enough," I said.

He looked a little surprised. I guessed he thought that his timeline would be enough to deter me. It wasn't. Some stories are worth waiting for.

"Second, you write the story as if I were telling it. A first-person account."

I nodded. "I prefer writing first person."

"Third, you give me the benefit of the doubt."

"What do you mean?"

"You might not believe what I tell you. In fact, you probably won't. I get that. Just as long as you believe that I believe what I'm telling you."

"I can do that too," I said.

"And last, you tell the *whole* story. That includes my history. You can't understand the end if you don't know the beginning. Trust me, it's for your benefit. Nothing is more certain to kill a story than an unsympathetic protagonist, which is what I am. At least I was. Maybe I still am."

"And if I accept your terms?"

"Then come over here and I'll order you another lemonade or whatever it is you're drinking."

We talked for the better part of four hours. Actually, he talked. I'd ask a question now and then for clarification, but a good writer knows when to shut up and listen. We stayed for dinner. It was after dark when I drove the late Charles James to a small Best Western in the center of Needles.

"How do I get ahold of you?" I asked.

"Give me some of your paper," he said. I handed him my pad, and he wrote out an e-mail address. "That's my e-mail. I'll get it."

"Thanks."

He smiled. "Tell me that after the book's published."

⋆⇒◉⇐⋆

We talked many times after that. More than fifty times in all. What was especially helpful is that he was an avid diary keeper and had recorded his entire experience. In the end, I had to wait only a little more than three years to publish his story.

This is Charles James's story in his own words. On the outside, it's a story about why a man walked away from a successful career and fortune. On the inside it's much more. It's a story about one man's search for redemption and what he might do if given the chance to live his life over.

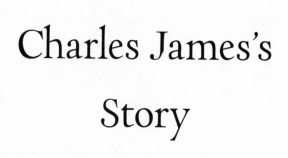

Charles James's

Story

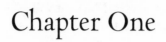

Chapter One

The well from which we receive grace is only filled by sharing it with others.

—CHARLES JAMES'S DIARY

SUNDAY, APRIL 24 (FOUR YEARS EARLIER)
St. Louis, Missouri

My name is Charles James. I have waged a fierce internal struggle over whether to share my story—the devil on one shoulder saying it would only serve to humiliate me, the angel on the other saying it might help others. If you're reading this, the angel won—though not without a few cuts and bruises.

That's not to say you will like me. You won't. Some of you will hate me. I don't blame you. I have spent a fair amount of time hating myself. But I ask that you might extend me just enough grace to hear my story. Not so I can excuse what I've done—there is no excuse for what I've done—but so you can see how even someone as lost as I was can find himself. Who knows? Maybe it will help you with your struggles. Maybe it will even help you find a little grace for yourself.

You might assume that my journey started the day I died to the world. But it started long before that. The day of my death, Tuesday, May 3, was just the day the tracks switched beneath my life. I'll begin my story a week or so before.

⋯≡◎═⋯

It was a rainy evening in St. Louis, Missouri. I was doing what I do—preaching the gospel of wealth to an auditorium of hopefuls and believers. There were about twelve hundred people in the audience that night, each attendee bought and paid for through advertising. There was a science to the numbers and a price placed on each attendee—$327 for each butt in a chair.

I took a last swig from a can of energy drink as the announcer boomed, "Ladies and gentlemen, the moment you've been waiting for, the man of the hour, the direct descendant of the legendary outlaw Jesse James, the incomparable . . . Charles James!"

Music blared as I walked out from behind the curtain, both of my hands raised triumphantly in the air. Somewhat appropriately, my theme song was Tears for Fears' "Everybody Wants to Rule the World."

I walked to the center of the stage as the crowd roared. I snatched the microphone from its stand and just stood there, looking out over the cheering audience for more than a minute, waiting for the applause to settle. When

I sensed it was starting to slow, I raised my hand. "Thank you. Thank you, you're very kind. That's enough. Now calm down. Time's important. We've got things to talk about. Important things. Vital things."

When the crowd had hushed, I said, "Henry David Thoreau wrote, 'The mass of men lead lives of quiet desperation.' There is one great truth in life that will determine whether your life is one of success or one of quiet desperation." I stabbed at the air with my index finger. "Just one. Do you want to know that truth?"

I paused for their response. After more than seven hundred presentations I already knew how they'd respond. I always did. I saw some heads nodding. Then a few brave souls shouted, "Yes!" or "Tell us!"

I looked at the audience in feigned disappointment, tapping the microphone against my chin. "That's not promising. I *saaaid*"—holding the word like a television evangelist—"do you want to hear *that truth*? Because I'm not casting pearls before a bunch of swine. Not *here*. Not *now*. Not *ever*. In fact, will all swine please leave the hall right now."

Not surprisingly, no one stood. Someone in the crowd shouted, "Sooey!" Everyone laughed.

Perfect. I looked the crowd over until they again quieted. Then, speaking in a softer voice than before, again asked, "Do you want to hear the one great truth?"

"Yes!" came the resounding response. "Tell us!"

I took a deep breath, feigning disappointment. "If that's all the passion you can muster for the one great truth of life, you might as well leave right now. In fact, you might as

well just die right now, because your life is going nowhere."
I looked at them for another thirty seconds for effect, creating a strained atmosphere in the room. Then I said, "All right, let's do this one more time. Last chance. I want to hear winners, not whiners. Do. You. Want. To. Know. The. One. Great. Truth. Yes or no?"

The chorus was deafening. "Yes!"

"All right then," I said, lowering my hand. "All right. I knew you could do it. Now you're sounding like winners." I walked to the edge of the stage, looking into the eyes of those in the front row. "This is it. Listen very carefully." I knelt down on one knee and softened my voice. "This is the one great truth."

The room fell dead quiet. You could hear a credit card drop.

"In life, you are either the butcher or the sheep. There is no in-between."

I waited a moment, and then stood. "You are either the butcher or the sheep!" I shouted. "Which are you? Am I talking to a room full of sheep?" I looked out over the audience. "*Anyone* who is a sheep, stand up and walk out right now. I don't waste my time with swine and sheep. If you're not strong enough, if you don't *care* enough about your life enough to choose to be an apex predator, to be a warrior, then go right ahead and join the millions of sheep outside this convention center. There's always room in their flock. Go ahead, I'm waiting."

Again, predictably, no one stood. They never did.

"All right then. You want to be predators. You want to be lions. That's good. But even lions must be taught how to kill. They must be prepared and tested. But lions have an advantage over you. They are *raised* to be lions. You, on the other hand, were raised, by society, to be sheep. To be timid and weak. Not your fault. Society *fears* lions. A world of lions is impossible to control. Impossible to slaughter. While a world of sheep is easy to lead, easy to butcher. Many of you came here today as sheep. The good news, if you have the courage to choose to win, is that you will leave as lions.

"What I'm talking about is change. Deep, personal change." I pounded my abs. "*Core* change. And change is coming whether you like it or not. Sometimes you can feel it, the way old people can feel changing weather in their joints. Change is *always* coming. Nothing is more unchanging than change, just as nothing is more certain than uncertainty."

I looked out over the audience, their faces barely visible in the dark, as the hall's spotlights were all on me. "Look around you. The wave is coming. Not just any wave, but a tsunami. Will you ride it, or will it rush over you, drown you?"

⊷═◉═⊷

It was the perfect segue into my near-death story. Every presenter I knew had a good "brush with death" experience, even if they had to make one up. I didn't. I just embellished it.

Nine months earlier, my now ex-girlfriend and I had spent the day at Flamands Beach in St. Barths, an immaculate white-sand beach where beautiful people sunned beneath skies as clear as the turquoise water while white-clad beach servants ran from chair to chair taking drink orders.

I had swum and bodysurfed for several hours and was just about to head in to shore when I saw a large wave coming. I swam into it, catching the crest. I soon discovered that I hadn't caught the wave, rather it had caught me. I felt myself tumbling through the water like a sock in a dryer. My tumbling came to an abrupt stop as I hit ground.

"There was a loud snap," I told the crowd. "As sharp as a breaking tree branch. My first thought was that I had broken my neck. It's remarkable how quickly your thoughts run in crisis. *This is how you die*, I thought. *Right here, right now, underwater, unseen.* I imagined my lifeless body washing up on shore.

"I was angry. Death wasn't on my to-do list when I got up that morning. It never is. But I was still alive, and I knew I had a choice. I knew I was broken, but I still had a choice. I could give up or I could live.

"At that moment, I decided to live. In spite of the pain, in spite of my body being in shock, I began clawing my way toward shore. It was only when I had got my body halfway out of the water that I passed out.

"I woke in an ambulance. They drove me to a small medical clinic where no one spoke English. I had crushed my scapula and broken all of my ribs. I was bandaged up and given nothing but Tylenol for the pain. That night, I flew back to Chicago and the emergency room at Northwestern Memorial Hospital. I'll never forget the doctor walking into my room carrying my X-rays.

"'You shouldn't be alive,' he told me. 'That's the worst break I've seen on anyone still breathing.'"

The audience listened intensely. It didn't matter that the story wasn't true. At least, not completely. I had been bodysurfing in St. Barths when I broke my arm. But that was it. The truth didn't matter, just the story.

"You're either living or you're dying," I said softly. "So what is it? The financial waves of life are drowning you. Every time you think you might get ahead, they pound you down again and again. Will you live or will you die? That's a question only you can answer right now." I took a deep breath and said, "For the survivors in this room, for those who choose to be warriors and apex predators, for those who choose to live, I'm going to teach you how to ride those waves. I'm not just talking about treading water, I'm talking about surfing those babies onto white-sand beaches. I'm going to teach you how to make money in your sleep. Who is with me? Where are my lions?"

The crowd roared. A half hour later people lined up with their credit cards, checkbooks, and hope.

Chapter Two

Sometimes the darkest moments of our past return to us in human form.

—CHARLES JAMES'S DIARY

After my speech, I swapped my suit jacket for a black turtleneck and put on my Ray-Ban Wayfarers. It was something I always did as I left the stage to avoid being accosted by fans or detractors.

I was walking out the back entrance on the way to my room when someone shouted, "Hey. Gonzales."

It was a name few people knew and even fewer called me. I turned around to see a large gray-haired man walking toward me. He was dressed in an oversize Tommy Bahama silk Hawaiian shirt with loose-fitting pants. Even though I hadn't seen him in more than a decade, I immediately recognized him. It was McKay Benson, the man who had brought me into the business.

The last time I'd seen McKay was in court, where he had unsuccessfully sued me. We hadn't spoken since then.

He hated me, but I had my reasons to hate him as well. I couldn't imagine what he wanted.

"Speak of the devil," I said.

"And the devil appears," McKay replied. "Good job in there. You've still got it. Mass mind control at its finest."

"I learned from the best."

"Yes you did."

Surprisingly, he reached out his hand to shake. I didn't shake, and not just because of my OCD. After what we'd been through, it didn't seem natural. He took back his hand, looking neither surprised nor offended.

It was surreal seeing him again. He had changed a lot. He was tan—not surprising, since he now lived in Florida—but he'd also gone completely gray and he'd gained weight, at least thirty pounds.

McKay was tall, six foot three, though he had always seemed larger to me on stage, like a heroic-sized version of himself. But that was then. Now he looked mortal and old and a little stooped.

He was older than me by nearly thirty years. I'd met him when I was twenty-one. He was not only my mentor, he was one of the pioneers of the seminar sales industry, the presenter we all emulated and hoped to be someday. The media had dubbed him the Godfather of the seminar stage. He was even the one who got me to play up my Jesse James connection.

But all that was before our falling-out. Even though McKay had lost his company and the lawsuit, he had already made millions, and rather than start over again he retired. His exit was a Florida beachfront condo, a thirty-six-year-old trophy wife (a former Denver Broncos cheer-leader), and a sixty-two-foot motor yacht he christened *Reel Living*, which he docked near Hollywood, Florida. At least that's what I had been told. I also heard that he now had two sons.

"What are you doing here?" I asked.

"I came to have dinner with you."

"Thanks, but I'm exhausted. I'm just headed back to my room."

"I flew all the way from Florida just to see you. You can spare an hour for your old friend. I already made reservations for us at Ruth's Chris over at the Hyatt."

"We haven't talked in more than a decade and you made dinner reservations?"

"You know my mantra: Name it and claim it."

I had to give him credit: he not only said it, he lived by it. "All right. When?"

"Seven thirty. I figured that would give you enough time to go back to your room and recover. Or skip town."

"I'll see you there at seven thirty," I said. I turned and walked back to my room. *Speak of the devil.*

The St. Louis Ruth's Chris Steak House was located in the lobby of the Hyatt Regency near the Arch. The restaurant was crowded, and the hostess led me past full tables to the back. McKay was seated at a small corner table lit by a single candle. He stood as I approached. "Thank you for coming," he said. "I gave you a fifty percent chance of showing."

"More like thirty percent," I said. "But I'm here." I sat down, studying his face cautiously. "How are you, McKay?"

"Living the dream."

"How's Florida?"

"You know. I never wanted to move there, but I turned sixty and that's the law."

I suppressed a grin. "You look good."

"If by good you mean grayer and fatter, you're right. How are you?"

I was surprised that he was being so congenial. Considering our history, I expected a confrontation. "Healthwise, I'm good. Always good."

"You can thank God for that."

"I'll thank science and exercise for that."

"As you will." He leaned forward and poured me a glass of wine. "I got us a Chianti, from Greve, Italia. You always liked the Italian wines."

"I'm amazed you remember that," I said.

"I remember a lot about you," he said. "The Italian wine, the Italian women. Who was that one . . . Sofia."

"Sofia. Or Sonia. They were both the same as the wines—full-bodied, intoxicating, expensive, and didn't last long."

He grinned and lifted his glass. "To Italian wine, then. At least you can always buy more."

We tapped glasses and I took a sip. It bothered me that I still couldn't figure out what he was up to. McKay was smart, and he played people like pawns in a chess game. The only way to beat him was to move first, which was how I had ended up with his company.

"So why are you really here?"

"We'll order first, then we'll talk."

He signaled the server and she came right over.

"What may I get you gentlemen?"

"Go ahead," McKay said, deferring to me.

I set down my menu. "I'll have the rib eye, medium well, the lettuce wedge salad, and your sweet potato casserole."

"Very well, and you, sir?"

"I'll also have the rib eye," McKay said. "Medium well, a small chopped salad and your lobster mac and cheese."

"Anything else?"

"I should hope not," McKay said. "That's enough calories for today and tomorrow."

"I'll be right back with your orders."

When we were alone again, McKay started. "To answer your question, for the third time, I came to see you. I certainly didn't come for the weather. It's April, and it still feels like winter."

I looked at him pointedly. "You still haven't answered my question."

He smiled and took a drink. "So, you're still working for a living."

"And you're still playing for a living?"

"I don't know how I ever found time to work. Marissa keeps me busy. Too busy. Never marry a woman a decade younger than you, you'll feel it in your joints. She's got me doing Pilates now."

"Just a decade younger?"

"All right . . . two and a half."

"But you miss it, don't you?"

His forehead furrowed. "Miss what?"

"The business. The cheer of the crowd. The adrenaline rush of the stage."

He took another drink of wine and said, "No."

I just looked at him, trying to decide whether I believed him or not.

"I'm telling the truth. I don't miss any of it. The rush, the audience. Not one thing. I thought I would. But I don't."

Sour grapes, I thought. "So what gets you up in the morning?"

He smiled. "Usually the kids. Starting a family at my age . . ."

"Yeah, I thought that seemed a little crazy."

"It is. But it's *nice* crazy. My only regret is that I didn't start earlier." He grinned. "You should have stolen my company from me sooner."

I had to force myself not to react. "The Godfather has been domesticated. Or is it Stockholm syndrome?"

"That's good," he said, chuckling. "Stockholm syndrome. You seem surprised."

"I am. It's like they say, there are three rings in marriage. The engagement ring, the wedding ring, and the *suffering*."

"It's work, you know. All relationships are work. But it's worth the effort. She has my back, I have hers. In this world of dog-eat-dog, that's not a small thing." An easy, content smile crossed his face. "How about you? Do you have someone?"

Before I could answer, the waitress brought out our salads and set them down in front of us. "Ground pepper?" she asked.

"I'm good," I said.

"Please," McKay said. "Just a few twists."

She lightly peppered his salad, then walked away.

"I don't have time for anyone right now," I said.

"And you won't until you stop."

"Stop? I'm just getting started. So is that it? You're trying to get your company back?"

He chuckled. "I wouldn't take it back if you gave it to me. Are you sure it's worth the money?"

"Is my company worth the money?"

"No. Being alone."

"Being alone isn't the problem. It's getting away from the crowds."

"Loneliest place there is," he said. "Crowds."

"Well, it's not about the money. I've got more money than God. I don't need more."

He looked amused. "Good. Then you're going to start giving away your packages?"

"Now you're being stupid." I took a few bites of salad, then said, "I used to think that money was the goal. But it's not. The bank register just lets me know the score."

"If money isn't the goal, what is?"

"The *goal* is winning. It's putting the ball over the line while everyone is trying to stop you. It's *my will be done, not yours*. That's the heart of every competitive endeavor. It's the heart of society. The goal is to dominate the other man."

"Like me?"

I just glared at him. I was considering lashing back when he smiled and waved his hand. "Sorry, that was a cheap shot." He took another drink. "You might be right. I'm not saying it's right, but you might be right."

"Of course I'm right. It's all about the win. And for someone to win, someone has to lose. You're the one who taught me that. How did you say it? Losers lose. That's what they do. That's why they invented participation trophies."

He breathed out heavily. "I said a lot of stupid things back then. Things I'm ashamed of." His humility surprised me. This was definitely not the McKay I had once worked for.

"Are you happy?" he asked.

I laughed out loud. "What kind of question is that?"

"It's a good one."

"Why wouldn't I be happy? I'm at the top of my game. Sales are up more than fifty percent over last year, name recognition is at an all-time high, and my last book clawed itself onto the *New York Times* bestsellers list."

"I saw that," he said. "Congratulations."

"And I just bought an Aston Martin."

"Which one?"

"The Vanquish."

"That's not a car, it's a work of art," McKay said. "Cobalt blue?"

"How'd you know?"

"I know you. But you still didn't answer my question. Are you happy?"

I looked at him quizzically. "Why did you really come to St. Louis, McKay?"

He sat up a little. "All right, I'll tell you. First, I wanted to tell you that I forgive you."

I just looked at him. "I didn't ask to be forgiven."

"No, but I offer it all the same."

I don't know how he thought I'd react to his offer, but I wasn't impressed. "I haven't forgiven *you*," I said.

"I know. I hope you will someday. Not for my sake but yours." He scratched his chin, then said, "The other reason is a little more vague. Even to me. I guess I feel responsible for you being who you are. I did, after all, create you."

"You sound like Dr. Frankenstein."

"If the electrodes fit," he said.

I laughed and took a drink of wine. "This monster isn't going down."

"No," he said. "I expect not." His voice was slightly softer. "But I would hope you would consider stopping."

I looked at him incredulously. "Why?"

"We've hurt a lot of people in our lives. Good people. People who still had trust in humanity. People with simple faith."

"We woke them up," I said. "We saved them from their 'simple' faith."

"It wasn't ours to take."

"So let me get this straight. You came to St. Louis because you think you created a monster and wanted to stop me."

"No," he said, shaking his head. "I came to help you, Charles. I'm paying you back."

I chuckled darkly. "Paying me back? You mean revenge?"

"No. I'm past that. Way past that. I meant what I said about you doing me a favor. I know, I didn't see it that way at first. I was livid. Crazy livid. You stole my world. You burned my house down, why wouldn't I be angry?"

"For the record, *you* burned my house down back," I said.

"For the record, *you* lit the match," he said. "But we digress. For years you were Satan incarnate, the great unholy traitor. Then one day I was watching Marissa push Trey, my oldest son, in a swing, and something happened. I felt something I had never felt before."

"Bored?" I said.

"*Joy.* That's when I got it. At that moment I saw the blessing of what had happened and, to my surprise, I actually felt gratitude for you. If it wasn't for you, I would have still been up on that stage tonight missing everything that really mattered or could bring real joy. I never would have known my two little boys. I owe you for that."

He looked into my eyes. "I had lost sight of what brought real happiness. I'd forgotten what real joy was. Sometimes in making our way through life we get ourselves so lost and tangled in the thicket of self-interest that we forget that our self-interest is much more than a flashy car and a fat wallet."

"The thicket is where men like us are meant to be."

"No, it's not. Trust me."

I suddenly laughed.

"What's so funny?" McKay asked.

"I figured out what this reminds me of. *A Christmas Carol.* Marley's ghost visit."

McKay smiled at the suggestion. "That's exactly what this is."

"So, you're honestly telling me that if you had to do it over, you wouldn't? You would have been perfectly happy with a nine-to-five job, kissing some boss's butt, driving a Chevy Malibu, and saving up for a once-in-a-lifetime trip to Hawaii? I don't think so."

"That's a fair question," he said, nodding. "I get to answer with the benefit of my career—the money, the open doors, the personal growth. I even met Marissa through my work. So, in fairness, how would I separate it? But around every corner there's regret. I regret putting off life and family and children. I regret the people I've hurt. I regret the marriages I've ruined."

I gripped my glass so hard that I worried it might shatter. "Yeah, tell me about it."

At least he had the decency to look ashamed. "Like I said, I have my regrets. But I was talking about the actual business of what we did. When people lose money, they lose hope. And when hope fades, so do marriages. Sometimes lives. Without hope the world is barren. That's my legacy—a wake of roadkill on the highway of greed. It's a nice little legacy to keep me up at night."

"You're forgetting all the people we've helped."

He smiled cynically. "Helped? We helped ourselves. As for our customers, few. Very few. And whenever we found a unicorn, we'd grab them by the horn and wave them around as proof of our veracity, but we both know that they're the rare exceptions. Half the people never even open the success box they just paid five grand for. And almost none of them get a refund. They just resign themselves to the bondage of paying a new monthly fee."

"Losers lose," I repeated. "It's what they do."

He shook his head, took a drink, and said, "I have regrets."

"So that's why you came all this way? To share your regrets?"

"And to give you some advice."

"Also something I didn't ask for."

"Yet, like forgiveness, I offer it all the same, if you'll allow."

I flourished my hand. "By all means."

"What I've learned is that the more I unplug from the matrix, the more I find myself. And the more I like myself. It's like the Australian aborigines: when they come of age, they leave the tribe and go on a walkabout to find themselves. They call it the heart song—the path of the ancients. And in this walk, disconnected from everything permanent, everything they know, they find themselves and who they are in this world and what they have to offer.

"I wish I had done that. I think everyone should do something like that. The problem is, in the rapids of Western society, we're just dragged along by the current, too concerned with keeping our heads above water to wonder where the river's taking us." He leaned forward. "Have you ever thought about starting over? Ditching the past and being someone else?"

"That doesn't work," I said. "The past never leaves us. It *is* us."

"The past doesn't leave us, but *we* can leave *it*," he said. "The past isn't us any more than we're the road we drove here on. It's done, except in here." He tapped his right temple. "But what we're really talking about isn't being free from the past, it's being free from the *future*. It's not the past that enslaves us, it's the future it's connected to. You pick up one end of the stick, you pick up the other. Sometimes you just need to chuck the stick." He looked me deep in the eyes. "So why don't you? It's clearly not the money, since you have more than God."

"I've never even considered it," I said. "I guess I'm just too entangled."

"It's not that complicated. Just walk away before it's too late."

I took a slow sip of wine and said, "I'll think about it."

He gazed at me silently, then an amused smile slowly raised his lips. "No you won't. Not until you're old and gray like me with a tire around your middle. When that day comes, you'll remember this chat and then take a drink and think, *What was that guy's name?*" He poured me some more wine and refilled his own glass.

"You flew all this way just to say this to me?"

"Just?" He slowly nodded. "I'm afraid so."

"All right," I said. "You've delivered the message. Your conscience can rest easy."

"This isn't about my conscience."

"Well, it's not about mine," I said.

He took a deep breath, then forced a smile. "So be it. So be it."

I tried to look unaffected.

"So what's next for the posterity of Jesse James?"

"I'm starting a new tour next week. The Internet Gold marketing package. And you? Changing diapers?"

He looked at me for a moment, then said, "I'm dying."

He said it so matter-of-factly that at first I thought he was joking. But his eyes assured me that he wasn't.

"Are you serious?"

"As serious as stage four pancreatic cancer." He breathed out slowly. "Regrets. My beautiful little boys will grow up never really knowing their father. Now that's something to be sorry about."

"I'm sorry," I said. "I really am."

"Me too."

"So that's why you came to St. Louis."

"I needed to set things straight before . . ." He stopped. "Doesn't matter. Nothing matters anymore except Marissa and those little boys. Nothing."

Neither of us spoke until the room felt very uncomfortable. "I'll get the check," I said.

"I'll let you. I've got future college educations to fund, and you still have more money than God."

Chapter Three

*I keep having the same terrifying dream.
If I'm to be engaged in nocturnal reruns,
why couldn't my subconscious treat me to
something that I didn't want to wake from?*

—CHARLES JAMES'S DIARY

MONDAY, APRIL 25

I didn't sleep well, something that was becoming overly common. Of course, my surprise meeting with McKay and news of his impending death made sleep difficult. But even after I fell asleep, there was no peace. I had *the dream* again—the same terrifying dream I'd had six times over the last few months.

In my dream I'm walking down a long, cracked, and broken road in the middle of a barren desert landscape. I'm walking west, toward a setting sun. I believe it's Route 66 I'm walking, or at least what's left of it.

My dream is apocalyptic. Something bad has happened, and there is fire on both sides of me, making it impossible for me to get off the road. There's nothing for me to do but keep walking. I can't see anyone but I can hear them screaming and wailing. Then I hear someone calling my name.

That's when I woke, tangled in my sheets, breathing heavily and soaked in sweat. *It's just a dream.* I took a deep breath and closed my eyes. *It's just a dream.* As usual, it took me a while to fall back to sleep.

A few hours later I woke to my alarm clock. I groaned as I crawled out of bed. I changed from my wet, sweat-soaked underwear into my exercise shorts and went downstairs to the hotel's fitness center and ran on the treadmill for an hour.

Afterward I grabbed a protein smoothie at the hotel's bar, spiking it with an energy shot, then returned to my room. As I was drinking breakfast my phone rang. It was my personal assistant, Amanda, calling from Chicago.

"How did it go last night?" she asked.

"We did six hundred K."

"Not bad for a Sunday."

"No. What's up?"

"Paulie called," she said. "He wants to change up his presentation. He's wondering if he can have an extra ten minutes on the stage tonight. What should I tell him?"

"Tell him he can have five if he can increase revenue ten percent."

"I'll pass it along."

"And make sure he lets Carter know about the time change in advance. Carter freaks out when things run over and I don't want to deal with another one of his melt-downs."

"Will do. Are we driving together tonight, or should I take the train to Milwaukee?"

"We'll drive."

"I have you booked at the InterContinental."

"What's wrong with the Pfister?"

"They're booked up with a convention."

"There's always a room. Pull the celebrity card."

"I tried. They really are booked. Overbooked, in fact. I'm sorry, if I had known earlier that you were coming . . ."

"It's all right, it's just one night."

"The InterContinental is nice," she said. "You also have an interview with the *Milwaukee Journal Sentinel*. The reporter will meet you at the hotel. I've reserved a private room in the hotel's restaurant for you to meet."

"Thank you."

"You need to be careful with this one. I think she might be doing an exposé."

"They're always doing an exposé," I said. "And I'm always careful. If I can't win them over, I crush them into dust and blow them away. Are you picking me up at the airport?"

"At two twenty-five, unless your flight arrives early."

"Great. I'll see you soon."

Chapter Four

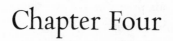

I have learned of two deaths in the last twenty-four hours.

—CHARLES JAMES'S DIARY

The flight from St. Louis to Chicago was only an hour, just long enough to take a short nap and write down some marketing ideas for my upcoming tour. I landed at O'Hare a little after two. I called Amanda from the plane, and she pulled up at the arrival curb as I walked out of baggage claim. She popped her trunk and got out of her car to greet me. As usual she hugged me.

"Welcome home."

"Thank you." I threw my suitcase in her trunk.

"Do you want to drive?" she asked.

"No. I want you to drop me off in front of the building so I can get into the office. I've got a lot to do before we leave for Milwaukee."

"No problem. I still need to pick up your shirts at the dry cleaner anyway."

We both climbed into the car. While I checked my e-mails, Amanda pulled away from the curb, taking I-90 to the Downtown Loop.

"So how was St. Louis?"

"I had dinner with McKay Benson."

She took her eyes off the road to look at me with disbelief. "Our McKay?"

"The one and only."

"Whoa. How did that come about?"

"He ambushed me backstage after my presentation."

"He just happened to be in St. Louis?"

"No, he came just to see me."

"That sounds painful. What did he want? A job? Revenge?"

"Actually . . ." I paused, stowing my phone in my pocket. "He's dying."

Amanda looked over at me. The news clearly affected her. "Are you serious?"

"That's what I asked. He has stage four pancreatic cancer."

"I hear that's the worst kind to get."

I nodded. "He said it's just a matter of time."

"I'm sorry."

We drove a little more in silence, then Amanda asked, "Are you okay?"

"I'm fine. Why?"

"You look tired."

"I didn't sleep well last night."

"I'm not surprised, after seeing McKay and hearing his news."

"It wasn't just that. I had the dream again."

She frowned. "The dream. How many times is that now?"

I shook my head. "I don't know. Five. Six."

"At least. What are you going to do about them?"

"What I always do."

"What's that?"

I looked at her and grinned. "Nothing."

⊷═◉═⊷

The Charles James Wealth Seminars offices were located on the eighteenth floor of the Michigan Boulevard Building in downtown Chicago off the Loop, just ten miles from my home in Oak Park.

Amanda dropped me off at the curb in front of the building and I took the elevator to the eighteenth floor. As I walked into my offices' lobby, our new receptionist, Candace, smiled at me. "Good afternoon, Mr. James."

"Afternoon," I echoed, hurrying by.

"Oh, Mr. James, your friend is here. I had him wait in your office."

I turned back. "Who?"

"Your friend. I'm sorry. He didn't say his name."

"I'm not expecting anyone." I turned and walked down the hall to my office. My door was partially open. I stepped inside. Seated in one of the chairs in front of my desk was an older, gray-haired gentleman I'd never seen before. He was dressed in jeans and a flannel shirt and wore round, wire-rimmed eyeglasses. He looked up at me as I entered. He looked tense.

"Who are you?" I asked.

"My name is Carl West."

"What are you doing in my office?"

"I'm here because my son invested in one of your get-rich-quick courses."

"Good for him," I said.

"No, good for you. He used every dime he had and borrowed two thousand from me. Nothing ever came from it. I told him to get a refund."

I noticed his hands were trembling. I suddenly feared he had a gun. I looked him over but couldn't see one.

"All our packages come with a satisfaction guarantee," I said.

"So you say. But you folks got it all figured out, don't you? At first he was too embarrassed to ask for his money back. But then it turned into fights with his wife when the bills got bad, so he asked for a refund. Your people humiliated him, made him feel like a quitter and a loser. They made it so difficult that he finally gave up. But that's your scheme, isn't it? That's how you finance your fancy cars and private jets."

"I don't have a jet."

"Neither did he. He could barely afford his used Chevy." He blinked rapidly, then removed his glasses and wiped his eyes. "We're just ordinary people, Mr. James. My son laid floor coverings for the Carpet King. He didn't make much but it was honest work. He wanted more for his family. He was married, had a new baby. He wanted to give his family a better world—the one you promised him. But it ain't real, is it?"

I could feel my face warm. "You need to leave my office," I said. I took a business card out of my pocket and wrote Amanda's name on it. "Have your son call my assistant. She'll take care of him." I offered him the card. He looked at it but didn't take it.

"I wish he could," he said, looking at me with pained eyes. "But he hanged himself."

For the next few moments his words floated unanswered in the tense atmosphere. The man again wiped his eyes and replaced his glasses. "You didn't just take his money, Mr. James. You took his hope. So he killed himself. You remember that the next time you steal someone's hope from them."

He stood. "I don't care about the money. I just want my son back. His name was Erik West. He wasn't just another fool in the audience. He had a name. And a family. You remember that name. Erik West." He walked past me to the door. "You're a crook, James. And someday you're going to pay." Then he walked out of my office.

Chapter Five

Crazy or crook, I am miserable.

—CHARLES JAMES'S DIARY

Erik West.

It wasn't the first time I'd been confronted by a disgruntled customer, verbally or even physically. It came with the territory. But it was the first time I'd been blamed for a suicide. McKay's words from the night before came back to me. *We've hurt a lot of people.*

"I'm not a crook," I mumbled to myself. "I am not a crook." I sat down at my desk. "I am not a crook."

I sounded like President Richard Nixon, declaring to the nation, *I am not a crook.* But Nixon *had* been a crook. Maybe I was too. Maybe I was just repeating those words over and over, hoping to believe them.

When you boiled it down, people had lost money—money I now had or had spent frivolously. Yes, they had given their money to me willingly, but in some ways it was no different than if I had held a gun to their head. Just like a common street thug, I too preyed on fear. Fear of loss. Fear of failure. Fear of being a nobody. And I was such an expert at it, I might as well have used a gun. Weapon or not, the results were the same. I was a crook. And a father had lost his son.

⋖══◉══⋗

A few minutes after the man had left, Candace knocked on my open door. "Your coffee, sir." She walked in, laid a napkin down on my desk, and set on it a Venti cup of Starbucks iced coffee. "Can I do anything else for you?" she asked.

"You let that man in my office?" I said.

"Yes, sir."

"Did you know him?"

"No, sir. He said he was a friend."

"Did you know he was really a friend?"

She swallowed. "No, sir."

"I've never met him before," I said. "Did you have any reason to believe him?"

She hesitated. "No, sir."

"But still you let him into my office. What if he had been here to kill me?"

She looked horrified. "I'm very sorry. It won't happen again."

"No, it won't. Pack your desk, then let Susan in HR know you've been fired."

Her eyes filled with tears. "Yes, sir." She turned around and quickly disappeared. I got up and shut and locked the door behind her, then came back and sent an e-mail to my HR director letting her know of the termination.

A half hour later someone tried the handle of the door to my office and then knocked.

"Who is it?"

"It's me," Amanda said.

"Come in."

"Your door's locked."

I got up and opened the door, then walked back to my desk as Amanda stepped into the office behind me.

"Why is Candace crying and cleaning out her desk?"

"Because I just fired her."

"That would do it," she said. "Pity. I liked her."

"There was a complete stranger waiting for me in my office when I got here. She let him in."

Amanda shook her head. "Who was it?"

"The father of one of our clients."

She sat down in front of my desk. "Not a fan, I take it."

"His son committed suicide."

She grimaced. "Ah . . ."

"Yeah. Ah. It's a good thing he didn't bring a gun."

"I'm sorry," she said. "And the man thinks his son's suicide is your fault?"

"Yes, he does."

"You didn't pull the trigger."

"No, he hanged himself. But I might have tied the noose."

She looked at me for a moment and said, "Maybe you shouldn't be going to the show tonight. You're not going to be any good onstage like this. Not to mention you're exhausted. We need you at your best for the upcoming tour. Paulie can handle your presentation."

"Not tonight. I'm stage-testing the new Internet Gold marketing package. I need to see the audience's reaction myself."

"And you're sure you're up to it?"

"I'm always up to it. The show must go on."

"It can go on without you. I think you need a break. Venice is nice this time of year."

"I'm doing my Harley road trip."

"And your dream doesn't give you pause?"

"It's just a dream."

"Maybe it's a premonition."

"You know I don't believe in crap like that."

She shook her head. "I know," she said. "If you can't touch it, it doesn't exist." She switched her attention to the package on my desk. It was a shoebox-size glossy black box with gold embossed lettering that read INTERNET GOLD. "Is this the new product?"

"It's the prototype." I pushed it toward her.

She picked it up, handling it admiringly. "It looks nice."

"At seventy-five hundred dollars, it should look more than nice. It should look like gold."

She set the box back on my desk. "That's what we're charging?"

"You know how it works. We'll charge what we can squeeze out of them. That's what I want to find out tonight."

Amanda was quiet for a moment, then said, "You've been under a lot of pressure lately. And you keep having these dreams. Have you considered talking to someone about it?"

"We are talking about it," I said.

"I mean a professional." When I didn't say anything, she added, "Like a psychiatrist."

"Yeah, that's not going to happen."

"Why not?"

"For one, I'm not crazy."

"You don't need to be crazy to talk to a psychiatrist. You talk to one so you don't go crazy. Maybe it would help you figure out why you're having that dream over and over."

"I don't need a shrink to tell me why I'm dreaming."

"Then why are you dreaming?"

I breathed out in frustration. "I have no idea."

"Talking to a mental health expert helped me through my divorce." She suddenly stood. She knew me well enough to know when she was fighting a hopeless battle. She walked over to me and kissed me on the cheek. "You are so stubborn. I care about you. At least consider it. I know a good therapist." As she walked to the door she suddenly turned back to me. "By the way, I sent a birthday present to Gabriel." When I didn't respond she added, "He turned eight last Friday."

"Yes, I know. Thank you."

"You're welcome," she said. She walked out of my office.

I knew it was my son's birthday because I had seen a picture of his birthday party on my Facebook news feed. He had been wearing a Batman outfit, the full-body kind with padding sewn in to look like biceps, chest, and abdominal muscles. My ex-wife, Monica, was cutting the Batman-themed cake. With the exception of Monica's best friend, Carly, he was surrounded entirely by people I didn't know.

I couldn't help but think how beautiful Monica still looked. Even though I hadn't talked to her in years, I still thought about her. Often. I know it sounds pathetic, but I made up a fake Facebook account to follow her on social media. After what I'd done, I knew she'd never friend me.

I put my head down on my desk. "I don't need a shrink. I am not a crook." I breathed out heavily. "But you are talking to yourself. You are definitely losing it."

Chapter Six

I'm not a believer in myth or magic. I understand so little of what I can see; I have no desire to waste my time on what I can't.

—CHARLES JAMES'S DIARY

Amanda and I left for the Milwaukee seminar around four, taking Interstate 94 north along the western shore of Lake Michigan. While I'd made the trip before in less than ninety minutes, this time it took us longer than two hours. There was an accident a few miles north of Evanston that slowed traffic to a crawl.

As I navigated the chaos, Amanda looked out her window. "You know there are monsters out there," she said.

"I've met them. They're called auditors."

"I meant in the lake."

"Every large body of water has a mythical monster. You don't really believe that."

"It's a big world and I believe there are still things in the water we don't know about. We've explored more of space than we have of our own oceans. People have seen things."

"Things? You mean like the Loch Ness monster?"

"Exactly. And Big Foot."

"And the Easter Bunny."

"Now you're mocking me," she said.

I laughed. "If life has taught me anything, it's that people are generally idiots. I'm sure they see *things*, they're just not what they think they are. Case in point, biologists proved that the water serpent sightings in Lake Champlain were really just otters swimming in a line. At a distance they look like a humped creature in the water."

"I didn't say they're all real. I'm just saying that I think there's more to heaven and earth than we know."

"Wasn't that Shakespeare?"

"Why are you being so snarky?"

"I'm always snarky. And I don't believe in anything I don't see and only half of what I do. The whole world is a parlor trick. Shadows and mirrors. I should know, I'm an illusionist."

"Yes, you are," she said, looking back out her window. After a while she breathed out heavily. "For the record, not every myth is false."

"Name one," I said.

"The Mapinguary."

I glanced over at her. "The mopping what?"

"The Mapinguary. It's a Big Foot–like creature in South America. There have been thousands of sightings by natives."

"Really, the uneducated, superstitious native people said they saw a monster. That's got to be true."

"I'm not done. The stories were so common that American anthropologists went down to see if they could find something. They discovered that every tribe in the region had drawn pictures of the exact same monster, even though many of the tribes had never come in contact with any other tribe. Scientists believe it's a remnant of the giant sloth, which is believed to have gone extinct thousands of years ago."

"Where did you read that, the *Enquirer*?"

"The *New York Times*."

I just smiled.

"What's the matter," she said, "cat got your tongue?"

"No. A Mopping Gory monster got it."

She laughed and shook her head. "You're awful." A moment later she added, "And there is a Big Foot. My great-uncle saw it."

Chapter Seven

Gone are the days of Walter Cronkite, when journalists were more reporters than fabricators. Today the only difference between fiction and news is that fiction, to be accepted, has to have a basis in reality.

—CHARLES JAMES'S DIARY

We arrived at the InterContinental Hotel around a quarter past six, nearly half an hour later than I had planned. The reporter was already there. She was an angry, anemic-looking woman with straw-yellow hair and a faint unibrow—like a Wisconsin version of Frida Kahlo. I could smell man-hate on her fifty feet away. She stood as I walked toward her.

"Mr. James?" she said, the tone of her voice pushing through a thin veil of civility.

"Sorry to keep you waiting," I said. "We got caught in traffic."

"I was told we have a place reserved for our interview."

"This way," Amanda said, stepping forward. "I'm Amanda Glade, Mr. James's personal assistant. Follow me, please. It's in the back of the restaurant."

"Thank you," the woman said tersely.

Amanda spoke briefly to the restaurant's hostess, then led us back to a room. The restaurant was crowded and I was impressed that Amanda had procured a private room for us. The reporter and I sat down at a candlelit table.

"May I order drinks?" Amanda asked.

"I'll have a scotch," I said.

"Nothing for me," the reporter said, even though I thought she could use a dozen stiff drinks just to loosen her up. She was one of those women who looked like she'd had a bad day for the last twenty years. Either that or she was walking around with a nail in her shoe. Maybe both.

She turned on a hand-size digital recorder and set it on the table. "I'd like to record our interview. Do you mind?"

"Not at all."

"Very well then; let's begin." She looked up at me. "Is this your first time in Milwaukee?" It was a softball question, a leading jab before an actual punch.

"No. I've been here at least a dozen times."

"And they let you back?"

It was on. I looked her in the eyes. "Is this the tone you'll be taking for the interview?"

"I don't know what you're talking about."

I continued to stare her down. "Either you're lying or you're remarkably obtuse. You think you're the first nasty reporter I've interviewed with?"

"No," she said. "Considering your reputation, I imagine you've encountered quite a few."

Touché.

A server walked in with my drink. She set it down on the table in front of me.

"Would you please wipe this table?" I said.

She looked at the table, which, I'm sure to her and the reporter, already looked clean. "Yes, sir." She grabbed a cloth from a nearby table and wiped it down.

"And right there," I said, pointing to a spot she'd missed.

She wiped it and turned to me. "Is that okay?"

"Thank you." I tipped her a twenty and took a slow sip of my drink as the reporter just watched me. "You were saying?"

"You have to admit that there are a lot of negative things being said about you."

"I don't have to do anything," I said. "Including this interview." I considered walking out on her but decided to stay and see if I could turn the interview around. It was a game of emotional chess. I like chess. I continued. "Show me anyone who has done anything of consequence in this world who doesn't attract criticism. Aristotle said that the only way to avoid criticism is to say nothing, do nothing, and be nothing." I took a drink, then added, "I've noticed you've mastered all three."

Her jaw tensed. "Some people have called your wealth programs a sham, and your ability to get people to part with their money nothing less than psychological rape."

"*Some people*? What people?"

She lifted a sheet of paper from her satchel. "People who have attended your seminars. Here's a list of a few of the comments I gathered online. It wasn't difficult finding them; there were hundreds."

Charles James is proof of P. T. Barnum's words:
a sucker is born every minute.

How can you tell if James is lying? His mouth is open.

Charles James claims to be the direct descendant of
Jesse James. I believe it. He's a crook and a bushwhacker.

That dude's pants must be made of asbestos.

She looked up at me. "What do you have to say to that?"

"The asbestos one was clever."

She didn't smile. I sat back in my chair, lacing my hands behind my neck. "What do you want me to say? Haters gonna hate."

"Do they have reason to be angry?"

"Your question is nonsensical. Any idiot can be angry over anything real or imagined. In the pool of clientele we attract there's a certain percentage who have never accepted responsibility for their lives. They're the ones who think they can get rich without any effort on their part. Some of them never even open the package they purchased or listen to the training."

"But you sell the idea that *everyone* can be successful. Do you really believe that?"

"Of course I do. Even you. Is there something wrong with that? Name an Ivy League school that doesn't promote themselves with implied promises of success. But here's the truth: Does everyone who attends Harvard walk out with a six-figure income? No. Just a six-figure school loan. But does anyone condemn Harvard for that? No, they don't, nor should they. Because rational minds accept the fact that every student has a personal responsibility for their own achievements. An education might give someone a leg up, but it doesn't guarantee success. So you tell me, how are we different from Harvard, or any college, for that matter?"

She looked at me incredulously. "You're really comparing your program to Harvard?"

"No," I said, shaking my head. "I wouldn't demean our program like that. What I teach is far more valuable. I live in the real world, while most university professors live in the cloud-cuckoo-land of academia. I'm the son of a poor migrant worker, and today I drive an Aston Martin. I used to get up early on Saturday mornings to climb into Dumpsters to get the food other people were throwing away. How about you, Buttercup? Have you ever climbed into a Dumpster for dinner?"

She looked back down at her paper. "The FTC has stated—"

"You didn't answer my question. Have you ever climbed into a Dumpster to get something to eat?"

The question ruffled her. "No."

"Then what do you know about what I do? Let me guess, Mommy and Daddy sent you to Sarah Lawrence

College, where you got your bachelor's in women's studies and journalism."

She looked at me with surprise. "You googled me?"

"I didn't need to. I've already met you."

"We've never met."

"We most certainly have. There's a dozen of you at every daily in America. Pseudo-journalists like you aren't made, they're pressed from molds. They're not educated, they're indoctrinated. You're not taught to think, you're taught to regurgitate the party line, then pat yourself on the back for your moral supremacy."

Her face tensed with anger. "Is that what you're telling the attendees of the Charles James Wealth Seminar? To think for themselves? Or are you doing that for them?"

"I'm not going to dignify that stupid a question with an answer."

She checked her recorder, then said, "You claim to be a descendant of Jesse James. Is that true or showbiz? Bear in mind, I do plan to fact-check."

"Fact-check away," I said. "I can send you my ancestry chart if you like. Yes, I'm a direct descendant. Jesse James is my great-great-great-grandfather on my mother's side. And yes, it's also show business."

"Tell me about your childhood."

"I already did."

"Dumpster diving aside, what else should we know about your life?"

I looked at her for a moment, then said, "No."

In spite of the tone of the interview, my response seemed to surprise her. "Why not?"

"That little boy has suffered enough. I'm not going to let your smug, elitist attitude inflict judgment on something you can't even come close to understanding. You claim to champion the poor, the underclass, the minorities. But when one of us actually succeeds, you show your true racism."

She adjusted her glasses. I guessed that she had had enough. "One more question."

"Yes."

"Do you ever feel guilty for ruining people's lives?"

I stared her down. "Do you?"

She turned off her recorder and put it in her satchel, then abruptly stood. "Thank you for the interview." She turned and walked out of the restaurant.

I was in no hurry. I finished my drink. When I walked back out to the hotel lobby, Amanda was sitting on a side chair near the concierge desk. She stood when she saw me.

"How'd it go?"

"Usual witch hunt. You need to vet these reporters better."

"Believe it or not, they don't usually tell me they're planning on attacking you. Besides, I did warn you that I didn't trust her."

"When?"

"On the phone this morning. I warned you explicitly."

"Well, it's done," I said. "Let's get over to the conference center."

"You still have an hour. Don't you want to go to your room first?"

"No. I want to see what kind of audience we've got."

The Charles James Fabulous Wealth Seminar had been going nonstop since nine o'clock that morning. I found Carter Sears, my show manager, behind the stage. He looked up as I entered.

"How are we doing?" I asked.

"About five-fifty so far," he said. "Not bad. Especially since the best is yet to come." From his unctuous smile I gathered he meant me. He was always sucking up.

Five hundred fifty thousand dollars was good, but not stellar. At my best show, last spring in Los Angeles, I'd brought in more than a million dollars in forty-five minutes.

"How's Paulie's new shtick?"

"Good. He went ten over—"

"Ten? I gave him five."

"—but he's increased sales thirty-one percent so far."

"Good. I won't have to fire him."

Carter grinned discreetly. "Are you ready for your new presentation?"

"I'm always ready. I'm just going to wing it."

"Nobody does it better," he said. "Good luck."

"I make my luck," I said.

Less than an hour later my theme song started to play and our announcer did his spiel. "You're up," Amanda said.

I stood up and put in my earpiece.

Carter walked up to me. "You're going to have to use this mic. There must be a short on the stage one. It keeps cutting out."

I took the microphone. "Is it on?"

"It's live," he said.

"All right. Showtime."

"Knock them dead," Amanda said.

"Don't I always?"

I walked out from the side of the stage as the music faded, replaced by the crowd's applause.

"Thank you. Thank you, thank you very much. We've got things to talk about, so let's get started."

As usual, I waited for the crowd to quiet. Then I said, "There is one great truth in life. One truth that will determine whether your life is one of success or one of quiet desperation." I held up a finger. "Just one. Do you want to know that truth?"

"Yes," someone shouted.

Just then, as I looked out into the audience, I saw the old man who had been in my office that afternoon. The one whose son had committed suicide. His arms were crossed at his chest and he was just staring at me. *What is he doing here?*

"Tell us the truth," the audience shouted.

I gathered my composure. "You want to know the truth?" I shouted. "Let me hear you!"

The crowd roared with excitement.

I looked back at the old man. He just stood there, glaring at me. Then I saw that he wasn't alone. Next to him was another man, a younger man. Except for their age, they looked almost exactly alike. It could have been his son. *His son?* His son was dead. Suddenly, every part of my body froze. There was a noose around the younger man's neck. Just below his jaw, I could see grotesque rope burns and purple-and-red bruising. The young man stared at me with black eyes as a malevolent smile lifted the corners of his mouth.

"Tell us!" the crowd shouted. "Tell us the truth!"

I was paralyzed with fear. Then I raised my trembling hand and rubbed my eyes. When I looked again, he was gone. They were both gone. Whatever I thought I'd seen had vanished.

A drop of sweat rolled down my back. I looked out at the audience, unable to speak. I could hear Carter in my earpiece. "Charles, are you okay? What's going on?"

The entire audience went silent. I slowly lifted my microphone.

"I'm sorry," I said. "I'm not feeling well." I turned and walked off the stage.

Amanda met me near the edge of the curtain. "What just happened?"

"Get me out of here," I said. "Now."

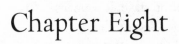

Chapter Eight

Does crazy know it's crazy? Does the fact that I asked that question implicate or exonerate me?

—CHARLES JAMES'S DIARY

Thirty miles south of Milwaukee there was another accident, again slowing traffic. There were multiple emergency vehicles, and the night sky was illuminated by red and blue flashes of light.

"Who's teaching these idiots how *not* to drive?" I grumbled. Amanda said nothing. As we neared the wreck, the traffic slowed still more. "Stupid rubberneckers. They're like vultures."

At a walking pace, we passed two ambulances. Paramedics were lifting a stretcher into the back of one of them. The body was completely covered by a sheet.

"It looks like people were hurt," Amanda said softly.

"They deserve it," I said, "for driving like idiots."

Amanda waited until we were past the wreck, then said, "No, they don't."

A few minutes later I said, "I don't know what's wrong."

"You froze on stage. It happens."

"Not to me. Never to me."

"I knew this was a bad idea. You've got way too much on your plate, Charles. You've got a ton of money at stake on this upcoming tour, you've been woken every night with the same nightmare, and in the last twenty-four hours you've been attacked by a reporter, found out that your mentor is dying, and been blamed for a suicide. That's too much for anyone. Even the great Charles James."

After a moment I said, "I didn't freeze because of the pressure." I glanced over at her. "I saw him."

"You saw who?"

"The man who committed suicide. He was seated in the second row, next to his father. He had a rope around his neck."

Amanda just stared. "You're scaring me."

"You think *you're* scared."

Amanda put her head down, covering her eyes with one hand. A few moments later she looked back up at me. "Charles, you don't have to be crazy to talk to a psychiatrist. She could help you put things in perspective. It's no different from what you do for the people you coach."

I was quiet for a moment, then said, "You said *she*. Do you have someone in mind?"

"Her name is Dr. Christine Fordham."

I drove a while longer, then said, "All right. Give her a call."

"I already did."

I glanced over at her. "You already called her?"

"She's not easy to get in to see. I wanted you to have options in case you changed your mind."

"When's the appointment?"

"It usually takes six weeks to get in, but she had a cancellation. She had an hour tomorrow afternoon, so I booked it."

"Tomorrow?"

"Tomorrow."

"What if I had said no?"

"Then I would have taken it. You've been driving me crazy."

The traffic had begun to clear, and we drove awhile more in silence. "Thank you."

Amanda put her hand on my knee. "You're welcome. I care about you."

"I know. You always have."

Chapter Nine

Perhaps our true psyches are revealed in much larger print than we wish to believe.

—CHARLES JAMES'S DIARY

TUESDAY, APRIL 26

Dr. Christine Fordham, the psychiatrist Amanda had recommended, had office space at a clinic about a half hour from my downtown office. I arrived ten minutes before my appointment.

The office design was clean and simple with bright, abstract art hanging on neutral-hue walls, blazing like Technicolor Rorschach tests. The lobby had sand-colored Berber carpet and a brown fabric sofa with two simple, matching armchairs, all situated around a white cubicle coffee table strewn with magazines.

Along the hall there were three closed doors, each with a doctor's name engraved on a brass plaque. Dr. Fordham's office was nearest the waiting area.

A middle-aged receptionist sat behind a desk in the corner of the room. She glanced up at me as I entered. "May I help you?"

"I'm here to see Dr. Fordham."

"Dr. Fordham's still with a client," she said. "Are you Mr. James?"

"Yes, ma'am."

"She'll be with you shortly. Please take a seat."

As I sat down on the sofa, my anxiety was through the roof. I arranged the magazines on the table into two neat piles of equal height, then picked up an old issue of *Sports Illustrated*.

I was still leafing through the magazine when Dr. Fordham's door opened. I looked up to see a woman dabbing her puffy eyes with a handkerchief. A thin, pleasant-looking woman I guessed to be Dr. Fordham stood behind her. She wore a pale herringbone skirt, a black silk blouse, and round, narrow-rimmed glasses. In a subdued way she was actually quite attractive, like one of those models who dons glasses and puts her hair up to look less appealing.

"I'll see you next Wednesday," she said to the woman.

"Thank you, Doctor," the woman said. "You're a godsend."

As the woman walked out of the waiting area, Dr. Fordham turned toward me. "Mr. James?"

I set the magazine back down precisely in line with the others, but then, seeing that the two piles were no longer the same height, I created a third pile before standing. "You can call me Charles."

She looked at the magazines, then said, "Charles. Come in, please."

I walked in past her.

"Take a seat," she said, motioning to a leather couch. "You'll want to turn off your phone."

"Of course." I took it out of my pocket and turned it off.

She shut the door behind her and sat down in front of her desk in a simple black vinyl swivel chair. She lifted a notepad. "Thank you for coming today. How are you?"

"Fine," I said, though I sounded a little ridiculous. If I was really fine I wouldn't be there. Maybe I should have told her I was miserable. *There's way too much psychobabble going on in my head.*

"Tell me about yourself."

"What do you want to know?"

"How severe is your OCD?"

"You noticed that?"

"That's what I do," she said. "Notice things."

"I've had it since I was a child."

"Are you on any medication for it?"

"No. I took Zoloft for a week, but it made me feel flat."

"Do you ever find it debilitating?"

"I usually don't even notice it anymore," I said. "What else do you want to know?"

"Are you from Chicago?"

"No," I said. "I was born in California."

"What part of California?"

"Near Santa Monica."

"It's beautiful out there."

"You've been there?"

"Just once. What do you do for a living?"

"I'm a professional presenter. I own a seminar business."

"I'm not familiar with that industry. What do you present?"

"We sell wealth education packages that teach people how to make money."

"How is business?"

"Lucrative," I said.

She wrote something on her notepad, then casually asked, "Do you like what you do?"

"Usually," I said, fidgeting a little. "So can we get on with the psychiatry stuff?"

She nodded calmly. "Why don't we begin by you telling me why you're here."

"I'm here because someone suggested that I see you."

"Who?"

"My assistant, Amanda Glade. She's one of your patients."

"*Clients*," she corrected. "Do you always do what your assistant tells you to do?"

"No."

"Then perhaps you came here because *you* thought you should come?" She just looked at me for a moment. When I didn't respond, she said, "One doesn't take their car into the mechanic unless it's not acting right. So may we assume that something in your life isn't going the way you expected or hoped it would?"

"That's an accurate assumption."

"Can you think of a specific time or incident that demonstrates how you feel?"

"Let's just say that I'm troubled."

"Troubled," she echoed softly. "That's a beginning." She wrote something and leaned back. "What's troubling you?"

"I'm not sure."

"Tell me what this *troubled* feeling feels like."

"It feels like I'm doing something wrong."

Her forehead furrowed. "Doing *what* wrong?"

"I don't know. Living. People are supposed to feel good. Happy. Fulfilled. Isn't that what mentally healthy people are supposed to be?"

"The measure of mental health isn't happiness or sadness, it's appropriateness. If you're happy when something tragic happens, that's not healthy. And vice versa. But you're right, our goal, overall, is to find joy."

I remembered what McKay had said about joy.

"And you're not happy?"

"I'm not even sure what that means."

She looked at me over the rim of her glasses. "You must have some idea or you wouldn't know it's missing, right?"

I nodded. "You really would be good on the stage," I said. I reclined in my seat. "So, you guys like to talk about dreams, right?"

"Dreams can be interesting. Some people believe that dreams are the subconscious mind's search for clues to their inner lives—that they are messages trying to be recognized by the conscious mind."

"Do you believe that?"

"Sometimes. Not always, but sometimes. Do you have a dream you'd like to tell me about?"

I nodded. "I keep having this recurring dream that I'm walking."

"You're just walking?"

"Basically."

"Where are you walking?"

"I think I'm on Route 66. Do you know Route 66?"

She nodded. "Headed west?"

"Yes."

"Are you alone?"

"Yes."

"Do you finish your walk or are you just walking?"

"Sometimes I get to California."

"What do you see at the end of the road?"

"Nothing." I shook my head. "I can't see beyond that."

She wrote on her notepad and looked up. "You mentioned that you were born in California. Is there something specifically in California that would take you there?"

I thought of Monica. "Not really."

"What was the first thing that came to mind when I asked that question?"

I hesitated. "Monica."

"Who's Monica?"

"My ex-wife."

She nodded as she wrote on her pad. "Do you ever see her in your dream?"

"No." I suddenly felt angry. "It's not about her."

"There are many things you could have said about California, and you chose to mention your ex-wife."

"It's got nothing to do with her."

Dr. Fordham leaned forward. "You're agitated. Why?"

"Monica doesn't have anything to do with this. I made my choice. I'm good with it." The doctor didn't say anything. Something about how she was looking at me made me uncomfortable. "You don't believe me."

"Your body language seems a little incongruent with your words. Usually if we are at peace with a decision or action we've taken, we don't become agitated talking about it. You obviously have strong feelings about your ex-wife."

"Everyone has strong feelings about their ex."

"Not everyone."

"I told you, she's not important." I stood angrily. "I'm done with this."

Dr. Fordham didn't say anything as I walked to the door.

"I said I'm done. I'm leaving."

"I heard you. The door's not locked."

I just looked at her for a moment. Surprisingly, she didn't seem affected at all by my outburst. "What do you want from me?"

"I want to help you. You came to me because you're troubled. I think we just found one of the things troubling you. If you wish to explore it, we can. Or you can ignore it. But that would be a waste of both of our time, since I think we both know that there's something about that relationship that's bothering you."

"It's not a waste of *your* time," I said.

She sat up a little in her chair. "Why do you say that?"

"You get your hundred bucks an hour whether you help me or not."

She took a short breath. "What if I told you that I was more concerned about your well-being than your money?"

"I wouldn't believe you."

"Why not?"

"Because you don't even know me."

"I know that you're in pain. That's all I need to know."

"What are you, a saint?"

"I'm human."

I leaned forward. "Look, I don't buy this humanitarian crap. I take people's money. A lot of money. Sometimes money they don't even have. I'm a freaking genius at talking them out of their money. Yesterday a man came into my office whose son committed suicide after I took his money." I shuddered as the words rang out into the still room.

"Would you like to talk about that?" she asked in a soft voice.

I hovered for a moment by the door, then returned to the couch and sat back down.

"That must have been very painful for you," she said.

"Who cares about me? I'm still alive."

"I care about you," she said. "And yes, you're alive. But it's not much of a life, is it?"

I thought I could poke through the veneer of this woman's pretended concern but I couldn't. This woman actually seemed to care.

"There's a reason I came to see you. I had something bizarre happen to me last night."

"Tell me about it."

"I was on stage, presenting in Milwaukee. When I looked down into the audience I thought I saw the man who had been in my office. The one whose son committed suicide."

"You thought he followed you?"

I took a deep breath. "He was with his son. He still had the noose around his neck. I looked away, and when I looked back at them, they were gone."

She jotted something down in her notes.

"Am I going crazy?"

She looked up at me thoughtfully. "I think you're dealing with some pretty heavy trauma," she said. "A man blamed you for his son's death. Did you think you could just shrug that off?"

"Yes."

"Maybe Charles James the successful businessman did, but your psyche didn't." She looked at me sympathetically. "That must have been terrifying."

I looked down for a moment, trying to control my emotion. "It was."

"I'm sorry," she said. "Let's talk about it."

Over the next half hour we talked about the young man who had killed himself. Dr. Fordham was very comforting and wise, and just talking about it brought relief and perspective. I was disappointed when the alarm went off on her phone. She casually reached over and turned it off. "I'm afraid that's our time for today. How do you feel?"

"Raw," I said.

She nodded. "I would expect that. I want you to do something. You shared some intensely difficult things today. That took a lot of courage. For the rest of the day I don't want you to think about what we talked about. Are you going straight home?"

"Yes."

"Good. When you get home, I'd like you to take a hot bath with the lights off and put a warm washcloth over your face and just relax. It will help. After what you've been through, you need to let yourself heal. Will you do that?"

I nodded. "Yes."

She stood and I followed her out the door. She put out her hand. "It was nice meeting you, Charles."

I took her hand. "Likewise. I'm glad I didn't leave."

"Me too."

"Now what do we do?"

"That's up to you. We opened a wound. We have more work to do."

"What do you think, a couple more sessions?"

"How many sessions is up to you and how you respond. A couple of sessions would probably be optimistic."

The vagueness of her answer bothered me. "How many will it take? Give me a ballpark."

"That's not really possible."

I continued to push. "What's the average?"

"I have clients who have been coming to me for several years."

"Years? They must be really crazy."

She frowned. "I don't use that term to describe my

clients. Some people have been through a lot in their lives."

"I'm sorry," I said, then added, "I've been through a lot."

"I believe you. I look forward to learning more about you."

"When can I see you again?"

"I can make time the day after tomorrow."

"Good. I'd like to see you as many times as I can before I leave on tour."

"Tour?"

"I'll be leaving for a series of presentations around the country. Twenty-one in all."

"Let's check my schedule." She led me to the reception desk. Two new people were seated in the room waiting for their appointments.

"June, would you please schedule Mr. James for this Thursday?"

The woman smiled at me. "Let's see what we can do."

Dr. Fordham turned back to me. "I'll see you soon."

I scheduled my next appointment for Thursday afternoon. As I walked out of the clinic, I felt both relief and vulnerability. The relief, I believed, came from confession. Maybe the vulnerability did too. We had definitely stirred something up. I just hoped that it would be for the better.

I drove home without even turning on my phone. I went upstairs into my bathroom and ran the bath. Then I undressed, turned out the lights, and slid into the hot water. Then, as the doctor had instructed, I lay back with a washcloth over my face.

As I calmed my thoughts, I found myself reliving the appointment. I could understand why Amanda was so taken with Dr. Fordham. The woman was good at her craft. Frankly, I couldn't believe what I'd just shared with a complete stranger. The illusionist had been tricked.

Chapter Ten

One man's holiday is another man's root canal.

—CHARLES JAMES'S DIARY

WEDNESDAY, APRIL 27

I slept well for a change. No nightmares, or at least nothing that woke me. My phone rang within two minutes of my turning it back on. Amanda's voice was frantic. "Where have you been? I've been worried sick."

"It's not a big deal," I said. "I just turned off my phone."

"*Just?* You never turn off your phone. Ever. I thought someone had killed you or something."

"That's a little disconcerting," I said. "Or revealing."

"What was I supposed to think?"

"Murder wouldn't have been my first guess. Besides, indirectly, it's your fault I disappeared. After my appointment, your shrink told me to go home and unplug. I was just following doctor's orders."

Amanda calmed. "So what did you think of 'my shrink'?"

"I was impressed. She could make a living from the stage."

"I told you she was good," Amanda said.

"Yes, but you also told me that tofu hot dogs were good, and I still throw up in my mouth whenever I think about that time I tried one."

"You're never going to let me live that down, are you?"

"No. It indelibly scarred me. So, what's up?"

"Are you coming in?"

"No. I'm just going to work from home today."

"All right. But I need to meet with you soon. Glenn needs you to approve the new video presentation."

"Just have him e-mail it to me."

"You know how he loves to do this in person."

"You want me to drive all the way downtown just so I can reassure his insecurity?"

"Sorry. How about tomorrow morning?"

"Fine," I said. "Wait, I've got something."

"Not according to your schedule."

"I made another appointment with Dr. Fordham."

"So you really didn't hate it."

"I never said I hated it. I'm going to see where it takes me."

"I think it will do you good," she said. "Just in time for the new tour. Can you believe it's almost here?"

"Yes."

"It's like Christmas. I'll talk to you tomorrow." She hung up.

"Christmas," I said to myself. "I hate Christmas."

Chapter Eleven

It requires peculiar acrobatics of the mind to hate God for not existing.

—CHARLES JAMES'S DIARY

THURSDAY, APRIL 28

I spent the morning looking over sales reports then drove downtown to Dr. Fordham's office. This time her office door was open when I arrived and she walked out to greet me. "Come in, Charles."

"Thank you." I followed her inside.

"Have a seat." She waited until I had sat down, then sat down herself. "How are you?"

"Still here."

"Was that ever in question?"

"No."

"Good. So, have you had any thoughts or epiphanies since our last meeting that you'd like to share?"

"I didn't tell you everything about the dream."

"You can tell me about it now."

"I told you that I'm walking west along Route 66 toward California. What I left out was that all around me there's destruction and desolation."

"What kind of destruction?"

"Fire, walls of fire."

She wrote on her pad. "You said that you were alone."

"On the road, I am. But there are other people. I don't see them, but I can hear their crying and wailing."

"This desolation is all around you?"

"It's on both sides of the road and in front of me, like I'm going toward it." I took a deep breath. "I think that maybe it's symbolic of my death. Or maybe it's hell."

What I said clearly affected her. She sat back in her chair. "Do you think you're going to hell when you die?"

"If there was such a place."

"Why would you think you're going to hell?"

"Dozens of reasons," I said.

"Pick one."

"Just one? How about because I hate God. At least, I would if I believed in one."

She looked at me quizzically. "I noticed that you wear a WWJD wristband," she said, glancing at my wrist. "I assumed that you were Christian."

I held up my arm, revealing the bright-orange band. "No. It's WWJJD: What Would Jesse James Do? It's a gimmick. We sell them at the seminars."

"Jesse James? The outlaw?"

"He was my great-great-great-grandfather," I said.

She made a note on her pad. "So back to what you

were saying. You said that you were afraid you were going to hell, but you don't believe in God. Is that correct?"

"Yes."

"Would it be fair to say that if there's no God, then there's no hell either?"

Her observation made me smile. "Now there's something they don't teach in Sunday school. God, the reason for hell. Kind of undermines the whole 'God is love' campaign." I shook my head. "I've never understood why people flock to a God who clearly delights in their suffering."

"What do you mean?"

"Do you believe in God?" I asked.

"Yes."

"So you probably think I'm sinful."

"No. I reserve judgment to God. And frankly, I believe that most people's condemnation comes from themselves, not God. But what I believe is irrelevant to your state of mind. What matters isn't even what's true but what you believe to be true. And from what you just said, you sound more to me like you hate God than disbelieve in God."

"That would be like hating the Easter Bunny," I said. "I usually save my disdain for things that actually exist."

"Yet you do carry disdain for God. You just told me that God, who doesn't exist, delights in suffering. You didn't say the Easter Bunny delights in human suffering."

"I'll put it this way. I'd hate God if there were one."

"So, hypothetically speaking, let's say there is a God. Explain to me why you would hate him."

"Because he hated me first."

"Why do you think that?"

"Because only an enemy would betray me the way he did. When I was a kid, I trusted in him. I read my Bible. I prayed every day for his help and protection, but he never once helped or protected me. This leaves me to believe one of three things: either he doesn't exist, he doesn't care, or he's sadistic. By not believing in him I'm actually giving him the benefit of the doubt."

The doctor made a few more notes on her pad and said, "Tell me about your childhood."

"That would take a year of sessions."

"Give me a synopsis."

"We only have forty minutes left."

"My appointment after you canceled, so we can go longer if you like."

Sadly, my first thought was that she was only asking so she could fill the time slot and get her hundred-dollar hourly rate. It was almost as if she read my thoughts.

"I won't even charge you for it."

"I can afford it," I said.

"I know you can. I just think it's important for you to know that I don't do my job for the money."

"How did you know I was thinking that? What are you, a mind reader?"

She smiled. "In a way we therapists are. We help our clients navigate their minds. My father was also a therapist. He told me that some of his colleagues made side incomes acting as fortune tellers."

"Your father was a therapist too?"

"Yes."

"That must have been nice. Having a father who understood you."

"It was nice. We're very close."

"My father was the opposite. He was violent and abusive. I was beaten almost every week of my childhood. Sometimes more than once."

"Would you like to take the next session and tell me about it?"

"You have a lot of cancellations," I said.

"Actually, it's fairly common in my profession. What we do here can be painful, so sometimes it's like the mind conspires against itself to avoid pain. Clients suddenly have appointments they forgot about, sudden emergencies, even migraines. It happens a lot."

"It must make it hard to make a living that way."

"It can be a challenge sometimes," she said. "No one gets into this line of work for the money. So is that a yes?"

"Yes. And I will pay for the extra session."

"Thank you," she said. She scooted herself back up in her seat. "You were saying that your father beat you almost every week."

I took a deep breath. "Yes."

"For any particular reason?"

"Because he could. I think he was always looking for reasons. Once he caught me with a *Playboy* magazine and he beat me unconscious." I looked down, feeling the pain of remembrance. "He almost killed me."

"I'm very sorry. That's horrific. Where is your father now?"

"He died three years ago."

"How do you feel about that?"

I looked at her. "How do I feel about him dying? Same way I'd feel about a cure for cancer." I expected a reaction but she just looked at me sympathetically. "You probably think that makes me a bad person."

"No, with a parent that violent, those feelings would make you normal. Most people would feel that way. I know I would. And this helps me understand your feelings about God. It would be hard to believe that God loved you yet let those closest to you hurt you."

Hearing her say this hit me hard. For the first time in my life I felt understood.

"Tell me about your mother."

"Her biggest mistake was marrying my father."

"Did she beat you?"

"Not like my father. But now and then she'd take a wooden spoon to us."

"Us?"

"My brother and me."

"How many siblings do you have?"

"Just a brother."

"Is he younger or older?"

"Younger."

She wrote on her pad. "Did your father beat your mother?"

"Sometimes."

"Did she ever try to stop him from beating you?"

"A few times."

"But not always?"

"No. A few times I told her not to."

"Do you feel like she betrayed you?"

"No. She was a lot smaller than him. She couldn't have stopped him."

"Did she tell him to stop?"

"It wouldn't have made a difference."

"She could have left him."

"It wasn't her fault," I shouted.

She seemed less surprised by my outburst than I was. "Have you always protected your mother?"

I regained my composure. "Yes."

"Tell me more about the *Playboy* magazine incident."

"Like I said, he almost killed me."

"Did you feel guilty about it?"

"Did I feel guilty for what?"

"Looking at the magazine."

"I suppose. I went to church a lot, so I had a lot of guilt about things. Like most boys, I had the usual sexual secrets."

"It's natural for a boy to be curious and excited about seeing a nude woman. I'm not saying boys should be given pornography, but they certainly don't deserve physical harm. And most certainly not as serious as you experienced."

"Is there a reason you're focusing on this?" I asked.

"Yes. Sometimes we carry strong emotions for abusers not just because they hurt us but because part of us believes we deserve it. Children oftentimes ascribe goodness or wisdom to their parents that they don't deserve. That's why children will feel guilty for things they're not guilty of. I'm trying to ascertain how much guilt you're accepting for your father's actions."

I nodded slowly.

"Where did you get the *Playboy*?"

"In a Dumpster."

"What were you doing in a Dumpster?"

"Foraging." A thin smile crossed my lips. "Now that's a story in itself. I spent much of my childhood in Dumpsters."

Dr. Fordham leaned forward. "Tell me about it."

Chapter Twelve

Some people use the Bible as medicine.
Others use it as poison.

—CHARLES JAMES'S DIARY

TWENTY-EIGHT YEARS EARLIER
Ogden, Utah

"Charles, get up. Pronto."

My eyes fluttered open to the murky, shadowed figure of my father bent over me. His coarse hand was on my shoulder, shaking me, shaking my entire rickety bed. "It's late."

Late. It was four thirty in the morning. But even as a seven-year-old I knew better than to talk back to my father. Ever. My ribs and face still ached from the beating he'd given me the afternoon before. He beat me enough without reason; giving him a reason was straight-up idiocy.

"I'll hurry," I said.

He clomped out of our room and down the hall in his

heavy, weather-stained work boots—the kind with leather laces and a steel toe. I'd felt that toe against my butt more than once.

"God loves me. God loves me. God loves me," I whispered to myself. I took a deep breath, then threw my quilt down and sat up, taking a moment to gather myself. My side ached from the motion, reminding me of the beating. I didn't remember why he had beaten me. I touched the right side of my face. It was puffy. *God loves me.*

I hadn't seen myself in the mirror since he came at me, but I didn't plan to. After one beating I looked in the mirror and didn't recognize myself. I looked like a monster. That time my parents kept me home from school for two weeks, telling the school officials that I had pneumonia.

I picked up the Bible that I had fallen asleep with and set it under the bed. "God loves me," I said one last time.

I slept with the book the way some children slept with a teddy bear. My mother had gotten the Bible for me at church. It was a dark-blue hardcover Gideon version, the kind someone put in hotels. In fact it said so inside the cover. I always considered the book my friend, even though my father sometimes used it against me, literally as well as figuratively, as I'd been hit by it many times. The spine was broken, and the cover had come off when he threw it at me from across the room.

My father was his own kind of religious, a law unto himself, claiming belief only as long as it served his needs or rationalized his behavior. Sometimes as he beat me he'd quote scripture. I hated those scriptures and even crossed them out of my Bible. Proverbs 13:24: "He that spareth his rod, hateth his son." Proverbs 19:18: "Chasten thy son while there is hope, and let not thy soul spare for his crying." Proverbs 22:15: "Foolishness is bound in the heart of a child; the rod of correction shall drive it far from him."

My father loved these scriptures, as they validated his cruelty. In fact, they practically made him sound righteous. What was bizarre was the way some part of me believed him. I came to a strange psychological place where I would actually thank my father for beating me and keeping me on the path to heaven, a path, I believed, that must pass through hell. I had to believe that, I think. The alternative was that my father hated me.

The mind does strange things to survive. I didn't know it at the time, I didn't even know what it was, but I had OCD. I couldn't make sense of what my father was doing to me, so sometimes, as I lay bleeding and shaking in my room, I would mutter strange things to myself. "Oh, uh. Um. I guess I'll hum." I would repeat this over and over, once for more than an hour. Then I heard a sermon at church where our priest told us to remind ourselves of God's love, even if we have to repeat it out loud. That's when I changed my mantra to "God loves me." It wasn't really a conscious decision, it just kind of happened one night after my father had beaten me for making too much noise when I came in from playing.

There was one other very strange by-product of my father's abuse. Sometimes when I heard my father coming down the hall with that certain step (I learned to tell by his walking patterns if I was going to be beaten), I would crawl under my bed. I found if I pressed myself all the way in the corner, he couldn't reach me. There were spiderwebs under the bed. To this day I like spiderwebs. I like the way they smell and the feel of them on my face.

As I sat on my bed, I looked over at my brother, who was still asleep in his cot on the other side of our little room. We used to sleep in the same bed until he started wetting it, and then my mother found a smaller mattress at a yard sale, which she covered with plastic leaf bags and sheets.

My brother, Mike, was only five, so my father pretty much left him alone—at least as far as going out Dumpster harvesting. He still got his share of beatings. This didn't surprise me. I'd been beaten since I was three.

That morning I wanted to sleep too, but it wasn't going to happen. It's just the way things were. I was always tired when we started our "route."

I heard the front door of our duplex slam shut, my father's truck door open, and then the truck's ignition cough as my father attempted to start it up. He'd had the rusty Dodge since before I was born, and it was already a decade old when he bought it. It never started on the first try but it was especially obstinate in the winter.

I held my breath as the starter motor whined. With each failed attempt at turning over, my father's curses and grumbling would grow louder. In the middle of last winter the battery gave out completely. My father stormed back into the house and started breaking and throwing things around, which included my mother, brother, and me.

After what was probably only a minute—but felt like an hour—the engine caught, and my father loudly revved it a few times as if to punish it for being stubborn or our neighbors for still being asleep.

I instinctively breathed out in relief as I pulled on the blue jeans that were crumpled on the floor next to my bed, the same pair I had worn the day before and the day before that. I only had two pair of jeans and the others were my *nice* pair to wear to church. Nice was relative. They were old and faded but didn't have holes in the knees.

I heard the front door open as I hurriedly pulled on a sweatshirt, then my coat over it, rolling the sweatshirt sleeves back. The sweatshirt was large for me, but it was winter and my coat, which my mother had found at a thrift shop, had a tear in one side and had lost some of its batting.

As I walked out of my room, my father handed me a piece of bread with mayonnaise spread across it. "Let's go. We're late."

"Sorry," I said, taking the bread. My father had told me that it was an egg sandwich, which, technically, it was. I didn't care. It was food and I never had the luxury of being picky. He'd just as soon not give me anything.

I walked out to the truck. It had snowed during the night and my father had already cleared the windshield. The truck door creaked as I opened it and climbed in onto the cold vinyl seat. The sound of the truck's defroster blasted the small cab.

My father glanced over at me. "Where are your gloves?"

"I lost them."

"Lost them," he said angrily. "We don't have money to buy more. Don't let me hear you complaining about your cold hands."

"No, sir."

My excuse was only partially true. I'd lost my gloves when three bigger boys had jumped me behind the school and beaten me up. I remember one of the boys saying, "Look, the spic's got a bloody nose. Better wash his face."

It was the first time I had heard the word, and I didn't know what it meant. Later, when I asked my mother what it meant, she just frowned and told me to never say it again—especially around my father. When I was older I learned that *spic* was a derogatory term for Mexicans. It's been traced by some journalists to Americans hearing Panamanians say, "No *spic* d'English." No wonder my mother hated it.

The kids at school called me a spic not because I looked Mexican, which, outside of my dark hair and brown eyes, I didn't, but because my last name was Gonzales—a name all the kids knew from the cartoon character Speedy Gonzales, a sombrero-wearing mouse. My life was doomed by a cartoon mouse.

My father's father was an illegal Mexican immigrant from Monterrey, Mexico, making me one-quarter Mexican. But my last name was 100 percent Mexican.

The afternoon that I'd lost my gloves, the boys had surrounded me, pushing me back and forth and punching me until I fell to the ground. Then two of the boys held me down while the other washed my face with snow. Afterward they stuffed my clothes with snow. One of the boys groped me as he shoved snow down my pants. Then they stole my gloves as they left me facedown in the snow—wet, sputtering, and bleeding.

I never told anyone what they had done to me. I didn't really have anyone to tell—at least anyone who would help. Saint Joseph Catholic School wasn't exactly a sympathetic environment. Corporal punishment was the norm and the priests and nuns weren't hesitant to beat their students, which begged the question: Why would you tell someone who had beaten you that someone else was beating you?

Home was the same thing. I couldn't tell my father. I could, but I knew better. He would only be angry at me for being weak. In fact, showing weakness was as sure a reason as any for getting beat. Once, as we got in the truck after church, my brother accidentally slammed the truck's door on my thumb. My thumb swelled up with blood and my parents had to take me to the hospital. I cried out in pain as the doctor poked a needle into the tip of my thumb to drain the blood.

When I got home from the hospital, with my thumb wrapped in bandages, my father beat me for "crying like a baby."

The reality was, no one cared that I had been bullied except my mother, and telling her would do nothing but add to her pain and feelings of helplessness.

That's how I lost my gloves.

⋆⇒◎⇐⋆

My father grumbled something about my stupidity as he ground the truck into reverse and pulled out of our driveway onto the dark, snow-packed road. Our first stop was behind the Albertsons grocery store just two blocks away from my home. My father drove around to the back of the store and parked in front of the Dumpster. He didn't kill the truck's engine, just let it idle as he didn't want to risk it not starting again.

We both opened our doors and climbed out at the same time. It was a routine I was used to, our weekly harvesting. The Dumpster had a plastic lid buried beneath a fresh layer of snow. My father pushed the cover up until the snow slid off, threw it back, then lifted me up so I was sitting on the edge of the Dumpster. I jumped in.

Peculiarly, Dumpster diving was the one time that my OCD need for cleanliness didn't kick in. The smell was always foul, but I'd gotten used to it. This one certainly wasn't as bad as some Dumpsters I'd been in, like when they threw out bad meat or a dead animal. My father turned on his flashlight and handed it to me while I dug through the refuse.

My father had given me two objectives for my hunt. The first, and usually the most fruitful, was to find glass bottles to redeem. There was a nickel bounty on glass bottles back then, and I could usually find a dozen or so in each Dumpster. I also kept my eyes open for another prize: dented cans of food. Sometimes there would be a big payoff when I'd find an entire case.

The process was like fishing. Some days there would be a big haul. Others not. I found all sorts of things. Once

I found an old man whose body didn't move at all even though his eyes were open. There were flies on him. It was the only time my father let me out of the Dumpster without finding something. He told me to hurry and get in the truck and he drove home without finishing our route. I wondered if he was afraid of being blamed for the man's death.

⊷═◑═⊷

Our first stop that morning was okay—not great, but okay. Eight glass bottles, three dented cans of Dinty Moore stew, six cans of sweetened condensed milk, and an open bag of jerky. This was just the first stop. There were six other Dumpsters on our route. By the fourth it would be light enough that I wouldn't need the flashlight.

"Why do we go so early in the morning?" I asked my father as we drove home from the last stop.

My father just looked ahead like he was thinking, his gloved hands gripping the steering wheel firmly, and then he glanced over at me, his eyes dark. "You think we should go after everyone else has picked through 'em? You think we should let everyone else go first?"

"No, sir."

"I'd say no," he said. "I didn't raise fools. The early bird gets the worm. We get there first. All those lazy good-for-nuthins, they get what we miss. We're just smarter than them."

His reasoning made sense to me. I just hadn't realized that so many other people were doing the same thing we were. I knew there was a lot I didn't know about the world.

I just hadn't ever heard anyone else talking about searching through Dumpsters. Still, peculiarly, his explanation made me feel good. It made me feel superior.

"We're smarter than them," I said. "We're early birds."

He nodded. "Damn right. Look at that haul."

The truck's bed had more than sixty bottles and forty cans of food. There was also a plastic cooler I'd found that was in good condition except for a scratch on one side, which rendered it unsellable.

As we drove back into our driveway my father said, "Put the food in the cooler and take it inside. Tell your mother she got plenty for dinner. And don't forget to scrub your hands and arms good. I don't wanna hear about you stinking from your mother."

"Yes, sir."

I piled the cans of food in the cooler and dragged it inside as my father drove off to work. He always worked Saturdays. He did gardening in the warm months and shoveled and salted walks in the winter.

⊷═◉═⊷

It wasn't until I was older that I realized why we got up at four thirty in the morning. My father was embarrassed that someone might see us. As I grew older I realized that he spent most of his life afraid that someone might discover who he really was.

Chapter Thirteen

We all swim deep in the river of our ancestry.

—CHARLES JAMES'S DIARY

My father, José "Joe" Gonzales, was born in Boyle Heights, Los Angeles, California. His father, my grandfather, had illegally crossed the border from Monterrey, Mexico, at the age of seventeen. He worked fields in Texas for three years, then went west, first to New Mexico and then to California, where he operated a fruit cart and married a woman who was half-Guatemalan and half-Filipino. That is where my father was born.

Raised in poverty, my father joined the navy at the age of eighteen but was quickly discharged after being found physically unfit for duty. He had been assigned submarine duty, where he discovered that he suffered from claustrophobia. He met my mother one weekend at the Las Palomas bar, where she was waiting tables to earn money for nursing school.

My mother, Fiona, was the cultural and physical opposite of my father. She was five foot one, buxom, with bright-red hair accentuated by the bright-red lipstick that she always wore. In spite of her bartending, she was a devout Catholic, and since my father had no religion, her parents would not allow her to date him. It didn't stop her from seeing him, though, usually late at night after her parents were asleep. Finally, in an attempt to win her family over, he agreed to be baptized Catholic.

A year after marrying my father, my mother graduated from school—she was the first in her family to earn a college degree—and became a nurse. Her salary wasn't much, but good enough that she sometimes earned more than my father, which embarrassed him. It was the same year that I was born.

My mother worked as a nurse until a year after we moved to Utah, when she hurt her back trying to help someone get down the stairs in a wheelchair and was fired from her job. No compensation. No severance. That's how things were back then.

While she was looking for work, a friend told her about selling Avon cosmetics. She joined the company. My mother was a hard worker and tended to do well at whatever she set her mind to. Walking door-to-door, she built up a sizable number of clients for her Avon business, and a year after hurting her back, she was making almost as much as she had as a nurse.

Once a month a big box would arrive at the house with her shipment of cosmetics, and when I was old enough I would help her put together the orders along with cellophane sample bags we'd fill with small tubes of lipstick and blush.

The December I turned fourteen my mother came down with pneumonia and was too sick to go out and deliver her products. She was scared. Since my father was unable to do gardening work in cold weather, things were already tight in winter.

She laughed at first when I told her that I could do Avon, but she didn't really have another option. Some boys might have thought it humiliating, but I didn't. I was spending my Saturday mornings in Dumpsters. This was practically high-class.

One afternoon after school, my mother and I put together plastic sample bags and I went out with a wagon, going door-to-door to deliver the makeup. I wasn't just making deliveries, I was on a mission to make money.

The women I visited were amused to find me on their doorstep. They smiled and thanked me, told me to wish my mother well and promised that they'd get back to her when she was better. But I wasn't quitting that easily. I told them that they would miss Christmas if they waited to order, and that I would wait for them to fill out their order forms. The women filled out the forms.

I wasn't looking for sympathy. I was there to sell. That's when I learned my first sales trick: power-of-suggestion selling. "Would you like some lip liner to go with your lipstick?" I'd ask. They almost always said yes.

The first night I went out my mother wondered what had taken me so long, but her eyes filled with tears when she learned that I'd come home with large orders from every one of her customers and even a few new ones. "You're better at this than I am," she said.

In many ways, that experience turned out to be life-changing for me. I'd gotten a taste of success in sales and I liked it. I was good at it. And it made money. My mother paid me fifty dollars commission for what I'd done. I felt as rich as Howard Hughes.

It was a pretty good gig until some of the kids whose houses I went to told the other kids at school what I was doing. They started calling me "Avon boy" and asking if I liked wearing girls' makeup. Not long after that I stopped.

Chapter Fourteen

We value most that which is elusive, which is probably why women were of such interest to me.

—CHARLES JAMES'S DIARY

I didn't date much in high school. I was interested in girls—more like obsessed with them. They fascinated me. I know that's not profound or anything—pretty much all boys that age are fascinated by girls—but since I had no sisters, they were truly alien creatures.

My sophomore year, in math class, I sat next to a pretty girl named Tina. She was petite, fair-skinned, and blond with radiant blue eyes. She told me that her parents had emigrated from Helsinki, Finland. I had no idea where that was.

Tina was not as shy as I was. She was sweet to me and told me that she thought I was "cute." At the end of one class I slipped her a note asking her if she would be my girl-friend. As she read the note a big smile crossed her face. She looked at me and nodded. I walked her home from school.

Tina was my first foray into the world of women. She was also my first kiss and brought out feelings that had lain dormant inside me. I'd usually walk her home from school even though she lived a half mile in the opposite direction from where I lived. Sometimes, on weekends, we'd walk up to the mouth of the canyon to kiss. Even though I was too young to think of such things, I wanted to marry her. I wanted those feelings to last.

Our relationship went on like that for about three months before one afternoon, as I was walking home from Tina's house, two pickup trucks roared past me, then pulled to the side of the road. The doors flew open and eight of our school's football players got out. Half of them were linemen and practically twice my size. The one exception was Stan Fuller, the varsity team captain and quarterback. He wasn't much bigger than me, but he had his posse.

"Hop in, Gonzales," Stan said. "We're going for a ride."

I was surprised that he even knew my name. I was a nobody. I was afraid. "Where are we going?"

"Just giving you a ride home," Stan said.

"I'm good. My home's not far from here."

"I know where you live. That's why we're going to drive you."

I stood there trying to hide my fear. "Really, I'm good."

"Don't be such a chicken," said a hulking, baby-faced kid with yellow hair. "We ain't gonna do nothin' to ya."

The way the hulk said it pretty much assured me that they were going to do something to me.

"Really," I said. "No worries."

Stan's expression hardened. He walked up to me and grabbed my arm. "Get in the truck, Gonzales."

I knew I had no choice but to get in with them. I thought of running, but they would have just chased me down anyway. I'm pretty sure all of them could have outrun me. And even if I had miraculously escaped, they would have just hunted me down at school.

God loves me.

They put me in the backseat of the first truck between two husky football players. My shaking legs looked like thin branches next to theirs.

One of them said, "You're that kid who sells makeup."

I didn't say anything, just compulsively tapped my foot on the ground.

We drove up to an isolated campsite near Shanghai Creek about fifteen minutes up Ogden Canyon. My anxiety grew with each mile. When we reached the campsite the trucks pulled up next to each other and everyone jumped out.

Baby-face grabbed me by the shirt and dragged me out of the truck to the ground and kicked me in the stomach. I couldn't believe how hard he had kicked me. As I struggled to catch my breath, several of the linemen lifted me up and held me while they took turns slugging and punching me.

The beating went on, as near as I could tell, for at least fifteen minutes. After one shot to the gut I threw up, which made everyone laugh and presented a new opportunity to my assailants. One of them grabbed me by the back of the head and pushed my face into it.

"Eat it, you Mexican dog. Eat your vomit."

They couldn't make me, but they rubbed my face in it until my nostrils were full of puke. Still, I barely made a sound. I knew that more reaction caused more violence. I had learned it at home.

After they had all gotten in their hits, Stan kneeled down next to me. "Stay away from our girls," he said. "White girls and spics don't mix, get it?"

"Yes."

"I hope you do, because this little exercise was just a warm-up. If any of us see you with one of our girls again, we're not going to drive you up here in my truck, we're going to drag you up here *behind* my truck. I'm going to tie a rope around your feet, tie the other end to my hitch, and we got ourselves a Mexican piñata. Got me?"

I didn't answer. Stan tightened his grip. "You got me?"

"Yes."

"Say 'yes, sir,'" he shouted.

"Yes, sir."

"Yes, sir, what?"

"Yes, sir. I got you."

He looked me in the eye, then threw me down. "You stink like puke," he said. "I'm going to have to wash spic puke off me. Let's get out of here."

They got back into the trucks. The wheels of the second truck spun dirt on me as they drove away.

God loves me. God loves me. God loves me.

⊷═◉═⊶

It was another ten minutes before I could walk. It took me two hours to stagger home from where they'd driven me.

It was nighttime. I was just glad my father wasn't outside the house as I came in.

The next day I told Tina that I couldn't see her anymore. She cried and asked why, but I never told her. I was too humiliated. Whenever I think back on that time, I wish I had. A couple of weeks later I saw Stan and Tina walking down the hall holding hands.

Chapter Fifteen

There are some who would gladly put you through hell under the auspices of saving you from it.

—CHARLES JAMES'S DIARY

Never believe things can't get worse. It was a Saturday afternoon and I was out raking leaves when my brother, Mike, walked up to me. He looked nervous but excited.

"Charles, come here."

"What?"

"I got something to show you."

I followed him into the house. As I walked into our room he got on his knees and reached under his mattress. He brought out a *Playboy* magazine. The cover was a picture of a naked woman sitting in a massive cocktail glass. "Look what I found."

I knew what it was, I'd seen kids with *Playboy*s at school, but I'd never seen one up close. I took it from him. "Where'd you get this?"

"It was in a Dumpster."

I knew it was wrong to look at that type of magazine, even though I wanted to. Our pastor had given a sermon on it once. "He that looketh at a woman to lust after her hath committed adultery in his heart."

I gave the magazine back to him. He looked at me with surprise. "You didn't even open it."

"You shouldn't have that. It's not good."

"You're such a goody-goody."

"At least I'm not going to hell."

⊷═◉═⊷

Still, the magazine haunted me. I was sixteen and had never seen a woman naked. Sometimes just knowing that it was under Mike's bed made me tremble. One night, after Mike was asleep, I got it and took it into the bathroom. I had just opened it on the counter when my father opened the door. I quickly grabbed the magazine.

"What you got there?"

"N-nothing."

"You got a skin mag. Give it here." I handed it to him. "Where'd you get this?"

I couldn't implicate my brother. I could, but it wouldn't help any. It just meant he'd be beaten too. "In a Dumpster."

"You know you're going to hell for looking at that."

"Yes, sir."

"Do you know what hell feels like?"

"No, sir. I think—"

Before I could finish, his fist caught me above the jaw, knocking me to the floor. Then he came at me like a madman, swinging wildly.

In all the times he'd gone after me, he'd never done so with the fury he showed then. I thought he was going to kill me. He beat me unconscious. I don't know how long I'd been out, but I woke alone and in the dark, lying in a pool of my own blood and urine. I tried to crawl up on my forearms but I couldn't take the pain.

I lay there shaking for several minutes, then flopped myself into the bathtub, fully clothed, and turned on the water. The water came cold at first, then warm. My entire body felt broken. The water ran over me, washing the blood and stink from me. I looked up through the darkness at the stream of water. I pulled off my shirt and my pants and lay back.

I must have passed out again because I woke to cold water. I leaned forward and turned it off, fighting the urge to vomit. Then I leaned over the side of the tub. My thoughts spoke fiercely. *They lied. It was always a lie. If there is a God, he hates me. He always has. I hate him back.*

Chapter Sixteen

*I don't know if I've chosen a different
path or if I've just finally started noticing
my surroundings.*

—CHARLES JAMES'S DIARY

Something fundamentally changed that night. Something deep inside of me died. Or woke up. I threw away my Bible. I threw it out back with the other trash. I would have burned it but I figured that it wasn't worth the trouble. The next Sunday I told my mother that I wasn't going to church anymore. She asked me why. I told her it was just a waste of time.

I started hanging out with Mateo, an older Mexican boy my mother had warned me to stay away from. She sold Avon to Mateo's mother and said their home was a bad environment.

Mateo lived six blocks from me in an even poorer neighborhood than mine. His father was in prison. Mateo had spent twenty-six weeks in the Ogden Juvenile Detention Center for burglary. "Juvie" he called it. From the way he told it, it was like going to college to learn a trade. He wore his time there like a badge—like someone who has run a marathon or climbed Everest.

He introduced me to beer, the Mexican kind, and whiskey and tequila. I also began smoking with him, cigarettes at first, then marijuana. He used some harder drugs, but I had enough sense not to go there.

Mateo had a pretty sister a year younger than me named Gabriela. She was as wild as Mateo and almost as streetwise. Sometimes she would smoke with us. She knew a lot more than me about boy-girl stuff. My mother had taught me the basics of sex, but with Gabriela, it was like a sport or something. Before long I was spending as much time with her as I was with Mateo. At least once a week we'd skip school and go up into the canyons to fool around.

I stopped caring about grades or school or even what the nuns said. I no longer cared whether or not I graduated. I got suspended from school for the first time after being caught smoking cigarettes on school grounds. My mother was disappointed in me but she never told my father. I think that after what he'd done to me for the *Playboy*, she was afraid he might kill me.

My life began to change in other ways. Just after I turned seventeen there were three major changes in my life. First, I had a growth spurt. I grew nearly three inches and put on twenty-five pounds. I filled out. I was a man.

Second, I discovered that I was a direct descendant of Jesse James. I don't know why my mother had never told us before. I think she might have been embarrassed by it. It came out one night when all four of us were watching television and there was a preview for a TV western about Jesse James.

My father, beer in hand, turned to my mother and said, "There's your kin. You gonna watch that?"

"No," she said.

Then my father turned to Mike and me. "You know your mother's great-great-grandfather was the famous Jesse James, the celebrated murderer and train robber. You boys got outlaw blood in you."

I don't know what effect my father hoped this would have on me, but likely not the one it did. For the first time in my life I felt like more than a cypher and a punching bag. I didn't know much about James other than that he was a famous outlaw, but I knew he was feared and dangerous. I wanted to be both those things. I went to the library and got every book I could on Jesse James.

What I read fascinated me. Jesse James's father, Robert James, was a pastor and a hemp farmer. He died when Jesse was only three, leaving Jesse and his brother Frank to be raised by their mother. When the Civil War broke out, the brothers enlisted for the South. They became Confederate guerrillas, which is how James gained his reputation as a bushwhacker, scalping Union soldiers and cutting up their bodies after they were dead.

James may have been the first criminal in history with a flair for public relations. He formed an alliance with the editor of the *Kansas City Star*, who published letters from James that proclaimed his innocence. In addition, the editor wrote admiring editorials that portrayed him as a type of Robin Hood, gaining James public popularity. It was said that when he robbed a train he would look at the men's hands to see if they were laborers. If they were, James wouldn't rob them. True or not, it made good press.

Jesse James was my mother's great-great-grandfather. Jesse James had married his cousin Zerelda (she was the one who cared for him after he was shot in the chest by Union soldiers as he tried to surrender) and had two children by her: a boy, Jesse Edward James, and a girl, Mary Jane Susan James.

Jesse Edward, a lawyer, married Stella Frances McGowan. Jesse Edward had poor health and subsequently moved his family to California, where the weather was more agreeable. They had four children, all girls. Their fourth daughter, Ethell Rose James, was my mother's grandmother.

For a boy who grew up hating his ancestry, this was a major epiphany. For the first time I had an identity of value—a birthright. I was blood kin to a legend. I was a James. And Jesse James didn't run from fights, he started them. He finished them. I believe that had something to do with the third and biggest change of that year. I stood up to my father.

⋆⇒◉⇐⋆

It happened on a Friday evening in October. It was what my brother and I called "shoebox night"—the night of the month that my parents took out the shoebox that they kept all the bills in. They would dump the pile of bills out on the kitchen table and begin going through them to determine what they could pay that month.

My brother and I hated that box. The appearance of the shoebox was a harbinger of pain—the lit fuse preceding a massive explosion.

That night, as usual, my father began heating up like a steam kettle, gradually at first, then growing louder and angrier until he was cursing and throwing things. Then he began hitting my mother. I shouted at him to stop and he took off his belt and came at me.

Something inside me snapped. For the first time in my life I didn't back down. My father hit me several times with his belt, raising welts on my arm, but its sting didn't even make me flinch. I didn't feel anything but rage and fury. I was a wild animal. I was Jesse James.

I went at him, slamming him up against the kitchen wall so hard that he temporarily blacked out and slid to the floor. Then I kept hitting him until my fists were red with his blood and he impotently held up his arms to block my assault. Then he began begging me to stop. He was actually crying. Like a baby.

Finally my mother, at first too much in shock to do anything, stopped me by wrapping her arms around me.

I stood back, tears streaming down my face as I looked at him in disgust. "If you ever touch any of us again I'll kill you. Do you hear me? I'm not afraid of you anymore, I'll kill you!"

He just looked up at me, his face covered with blood and his nose broken, shaking with fear. I had heard it said that most bullies were cowards, but it had never occurred to me just how much of a coward my father was.

I ran out of the house. When I returned home six hours later, the house was dark and quiet. As I got into bed my brother told me that my father had sobbed for nearly an hour.

My father left for work early the next morning before I woke. In fact it was nearly three days before I saw him again. I prepared for another assault, but he just cowered. He never touched me again.

Chapter Seventeen

The throne is cracked, the scepter broken.
The king has fallen.

—CHARLES JAMES'S DIARY

There is a scripture in the Book of Isaiah that reads, "Those who see you will gaze at you, Lucifer, they will ponder over you, saying, 'Is this the man who made the earth tremble, who shook kingdoms?'"

I suppose, in my realm, in my kingdom, this passage described my father. And now he was fallen. Still, the biggest change in my relationships wasn't with my father but with God. Just like my father, I had moved on. I had tried to be good and put my faith in the merciful and loving God they preached about at my mother's church, and I had suffered for it. From my experience, God was neither merciful nor loving, and he sure as hell wasn't going to protect me. I had to do that. The message from the universe was crystal clear: believe in yourself, because God doesn't care. I adopted a new mantra: There is no God but me.

Although I appeared confident, deep inside I was terrified. It's bizarre to say this but, in a way, having an abusive father created a twisted sense of security. Perhaps, subconsciously, I believed that if he could beat me, he could also protect me. But now that my father was humbled and broken, so was our home. It always had been broken, but now there was no longer the illusion of stability. The foundation had crumbled. The king had been dethroned.

I suppose that's why I had to leave. Not just home, but everything: family, school, Utah. I figured there had to be something better out there. I decided to go to California.

It was a Saturday afternoon, just six weeks before my eighteenth birthday, that I decided to leave. I had spent the morning at Mateo's, then came home and packed my school backpack with two pairs of jeans, three T-shirts, two pairs of briefs and socks, some soap, a diary I had found in a Dumpster, and a pen. I also brought a switchblade that Mateo had given me when I told him I was leaving. "When you get to L.A. look up the Sureños gang," he said. "They're the Mexican Mafia. Any gang with a thirteen in their name is Sureños. They'll take care of you."

I had no plans to join a street gang. I planned to make it on my own, even though I had only about $180, money I'd mostly made helping neighbors doing yard work.

Call it naiveté or youthful ignorance, but I wasn't afraid. Some people, mountain men, knew how to survive in the wilderness. I knew how to survive in the urban wilderness. I was a master at city survival. I could live out of Dumpsters if I had to. Even in poor places, people threw out things that were still good. I figured that would be true anywhere.

My brother walked into the room as I was finishing packing. "What are you doing?"

"Leaving," I said without looking up.

"Leaving? Where?"

"I don't know."

"For how long?"

"Forever."

"Why?" I looked up at him. He looked afraid. "This is our home."

"This is nothing, bro. This is a dump."

"You can't leave me," he said.

I picked up my backpack. "I have to."

He stood there looking at me, crying. I hated that. I'd seen him take heavy beatings from my father without crying. What I was doing must have hurt him more than a beating. That made me feel sick to my stomach.

"Stop crying. You're not a baby."

"Please don't go."

"There's nothing here."

"There's me."

"I'm sorry." I really did feel sorry. I would miss him, but I pushed away the emotion. "I have to go."

I never said good-bye to my parents. I never regretted not speaking to my father. I'd said all I needed to say to him and he'd said to me way more than I needed to hear. I almost told my mother; I wanted to but decided that it wasn't an option. I knew that she could still make me stay.

The Ogden Greyhound station was about three and a half miles from our home. I walked it in less than an hour. I had never been there before. The station wasn't crowded. There were fewer than thirty people inside, most sitting on the benches with a few sprawled out along rows of seats, sleeping. The floor was dirty and littered with trash.

Posted on the wall above the ticket windows was a listing of the bus arrival and departure times. There was a bus leaving for Los Angeles, California, at 4:55 p.m. and arriving in L.A. at 8:25 a.m. with just one transfer, in Las Vegas. I don't know what initially drew me to California. Maybe because my mother spoke so fondly of the time she lived there or maybe because I was born there. Maybe it was just in my blood.

I bought a one-way ticket for $69.99, shoved it deep into my pants pocket, and walked down to a convenience store on the same block and bought a couple of Snickers candy bars, a can of Dr Pepper, and two hot dogs, which I buried in the free chili and cheese sauce that came with them. Then I walked back to the station to wait for my bus.

I spread napkins down on an unoccupied bench on the east side of the station and sat. I figured it was unoccupied because someone had thrown up on the ground at one end of it and it stank. Stink didn't bother me. (A childhood in Dumpsters will do that.) I didn't care as much about the stink as I did some of the weird-looking people around me. One disheveled man kept turning around and shouting, "Quit following me!" even though there was no one behind him. I could put up with the smell if it kept everyone away.

After I finished eating my hot dogs I rearranged the

napkins and sat back on the bench and watched people come and go. As the day went on, the station grew busier and more crowded. A few times I saw parents sending off their children. The parents were emotional, the mothers crying, even one of the fathers. The scene was foreign to me. I wondered how often they beat their children.

Then my mind started wandering through a labyrinth of unknowns. I wondered if I would ever see my family again. I wondered if my father would start beating everyone again. I wondered how long it would be until my brother stood up for himself as I had. What if he didn't? He had always been softer than me.

I wondered if he had already told my parents that I'd left. *What if they came to get me? What would I do?* I dismissed the thought. It would never happen.

I've come to believe that before any major life change there's a crisis in faith—the flash of doubt before one hurls oneself into the unknown. For just a moment I considered going back home as a scared voice chattered endlessly: *What are you doing? You're going to die out there. Better to stay with what you know.*

I pulled the bus ticket from my pocket and fingered it before folding it and putting it back. I just had to remind myself that there was no home to go back to. Home had left me long before I had left it.

It wasn't just my home I was leaving behind. I left my father's name as well. From that moment on, I decided I would call myself Charles James.

Chapter Eighteen

It takes great courage to wear kindness as if one had never been hurt.

—CHARLES JAMES'S DIARY

The drive to Los Angeles was fifteen and a half hours, almost completely south along I-15, passing through Salt Lake City, St. George, Las Vegas, and Barstow to San Bernardino, where we finally left I-15 traveling west on I-10, all the way to Santa Monica and the Pacific Ocean.

I was one of just seven people getting on the bus in Ogden. Many of them had big suitcases and travel bags, which the driver stowed beneath the bus. I had only my backpack.

I walked on, handing my ticket to the driver. There were a couple dozen people already seated, looking tired and bored. A few of them glanced up at me as I walked down the aisle. I walked to the back of the bus, where there were fewer people. I still didn't want to sit by anyone.

I sat down in the last row on the left side of the bus. There was a young woman sitting alone across the aisle from me. She looked like she was about my age or maybe a year older. She was pretty, with large green eyes, a narrow face, and long brown hair. Even more than pretty, she looked friendly.

I put my pack on the aisle seat and sat down next to the window. After I'd settled in, I glanced back over at the young woman. She was looking at me and smiled. So far she was the only one I had seen on the bus who didn't look like they were in pain. I'm not exaggerating. I could have been sitting in the waiting room of a dentist's office for all the joy that surrounded me. Of course, I wasn't little Miss Sunshine myself. I shyly acknowledged her smile with a nod, then looked out the window.

Just a few minutes later I heard the pneumatic door shut and the bus's brakes release. The bus slowly backed out of the parking space, stopped, and lurched forward. My new life had begun.

Outside of moving to Utah as an infant, I had never traveled more than thirty miles from home—a fact that, for the first time, struck me as significant as the scenery around me became foreign.

My thoughts went back to my brother's sadness. I wondered how he would fare. I decided that I would send him a postcard after I was in California, just to let them know I was there and what I was doing, whatever that was.

My thoughts were interrupted by a soft voice. "Want some chocolate?" The young woman held out a Hershey's chocolate bar.

"I'm okay."

She cocked her head. "It's just chocolate. You don't like chocolate?"

"I like chocolate."

"Then have some."

"Okay." I reached over and she broke off a square and handed it to me. "Thanks," I said.

She slid to the edge of her seat to be closer to me. "You're welcome. I've got all sorts of snacks in here if you're hungry. I even baked some chocolate chip cookies. It's a long ride. More than fifteen hours from here."

"Thanks."

"Where are you headed?"

"Los Angeles. Isn't everyone on the bus going to Los Angeles?"

"No. There are stops all along the way. This route just ends in Los Angeles."

"Are you going to Los Angeles?" I asked.

She nodded. "Where in Los Angeles are you going?"

"What do you mean?"

"Los Angeles is big. There's a lot of different suburbs."

"I don't know yet," I said. "Are you from Utah?"

"No. I'm just coming back from Idaho. I'm from Culver City. That's in Los Angeles."

"What's it like?"

"Culver City?"

"California."

"You've never been there?"

"I was born there, but we moved when I was a baby, so I don't remember anything."

"It's nice. I mean, it's crowded and you got your traffic and crime, but there are a lot of palm trees and nice beaches. The weather's almost always nice. A lot of the areas around me are affluent."

"What's affluent?" I asked.

She smiled. "Affluent? It means it's rich. There are a lot of rich people in California."

"Oh," I said. A moment later I asked, "Are you . . . affluent?"

She laughed. "Would I be riding the bus if I were?"

"I don't know."

"No. I'd take an airplane."

I nodded. "Affluent."

"I'm Monica," she said, extending her hand. "Like Santa Monica. What's your name?"

"I'm Charles James."

"Is Charles James your first name or is James your last name?"

"It's my last name. Like Jesse James."

"Oh. Any relation?"

"Yeah. He's my great-great-great-grandfather."

"That's cool," she said. "I once tried to see if I was related to anyone famous. I'm not."

"Everyone probably is somewhere."

"Maybe. But if I was, I think it would be more like my great-great-great-great-grandmother was a house wench to the queen of England." She laughed. She had a pretty laugh. "It's just good we're not in those days anymore."

Less than an hour later the bus made a stop in Salt

Lake City. It was already dark outside. The city had the tallest buildings I'd ever seen. About a third of the passengers got off and more than double that got on. I was glad that no one sat next to Monica, though a few of the guys looked like they were about to. No one looked at me. I think I scared them.

We continued south along I-15 for another four hours. A little after ten we stopped at a gas station food-mart for a dinner break. The building was about the only thing in the town.

"Where are we?" I asked.

"Parowan. It's a really small town. Want to get something to eat?"

"Sure," I said.

"Take your pack. You don't want your stuff stolen."

I stood and swung my pack over my shoulder, then followed Monica off the bus. The driver was standing just outside smoking a cigarette. He blew out a cloud of smoke and said, "You've got fifteen minutes."

There was a Subway sandwich shop connected to the gas station. Monica used the restroom, then met me in line. I got a ham and cheese sandwich. She got something Italian. We didn't have time to stay and eat, so we carried our sandwiches over to the food-mart and bought a gallon jug of water, some toffee-covered peanuts, and a liter bottle of Coke. We took everything back to the bus.

We must have been the last ones to return, because when the driver saw us coming, he threw down his cigarette, climbed inside, and started the bus. He immediately closed the door behind us. We went back to where we'd been sitting.

"The next stop is Las Vegas," Monica said. "We change buses there."

"Do I need a new ticket?" I asked.

"No. Just the one you have." She looked at me. "What are you going to do when you get to California?"

"Find a job."

"What do you do?"

"Whatever I can. I'm a hard worker."

"Have you ever done yard work?"

"Yeah. A lot. My father is a gardener."

"That's good. My girlfriend's brother owns a landscaping company. He's always looking for help. You won't get rich working for him, but it's not bad. I think he starts his employees at twelve dollars an hour."

Twelve dollars an hour sounded like a fortune to me. No one I knew got paid that much. Not even my father. "Twelve dollars?"

"Like I said, you won't get rich working for him, but it's more than flipping burgers somewhere for minimum wage."

"Do you work?" I asked.

She nodded. "I work at a retirement home. I'm a CNA."

"What's that?"

"It stands for Certified Nursing Assistant."

"That sounds important," I said.

She laughed. "If changing old people's diapers is important."

I thought for a moment, then said, "It is for the old people."

⋆═◉═⋆

Our bus rolled into Las Vegas a little after one in the morning. I had never seen anything like the city before—a galaxy of bright, flashing lights, teeming crowds, and shiny expensive cars. Even at one in the morning, the streets were more crowded than Ogden at rush hour.

The driver turned off the bus and announced over the P.A. system that this stop was the end of the line and everyone needed to get off. Everyone stood and gathered their things, though a few people had to be woken up. One guy was really confused. I heard him ask if we were in Phoenix.

The Las Vegas bus station was very different from the one in Ogden. It was nice, for one thing. Clean. It was open to the air and there were palm trees around it, something I hadn't seen outside of a magazine or television.

I waited for Monica as she got her luggage from the bus's storage. The weather was much warmer and more humid than it was in Ogden. I took off my hoodie. I was already sweating through it.

"Is it this hot in California?" I asked Monica.

"No," she said. "It's warmer than Utah, but not Las Vegas. This is the desert."

Buses filled with tourists kept arriving at the station. For most of them Vegas must have been their final destination: they were acting excited and uninhibited, like they were drunk or something. People kept saying, "What happens in Vegas stays in Vegas." Whatever that meant. I wanted to leave.

"Do you know where we're going?" I asked Monica.

"Yes. Just follow me."

Monica had two bags, which I helped her carry. We walked past four or five buses until we came to one with a sign in the window that read LOS ANGELES / SANTA MONICA. There was a line of people boarding.

"This is it," she said. "It's always more crowded than the first one. I've got to give them my bags. Why don't you get on and save us a seat so we can sit together?"

"Okay," I said, glad that she still wanted to sit by me. I got in line and boarded the bus. Like Monica said, it was more full than the one we had left and there were only a couple of seats near the back still vacant. I grabbed a seat and put my pack on the seat next to it. A few minutes later Monica walked down the aisle. I raised my hand so she'd see me. When she got to me I said, "Do you want the window?"

"No. You can have it."

I slid across the seat and she sat down next to me, stowing her things under the seat in front of her.

"I'm glad you're here," she said. "I might have ended up sitting next to some stinky fat guy. The first time I was on this bus, this old guy with hair growing out of his ears sat next to me. I fell asleep, and when I woke up he was touching me."

"Where?" I asked. She touched her chest. "What did you do?"

"I screamed. The bus driver stopped the bus and made the guy sit up next to him. Then he made him get off the bus at the next city."

"He probably wasn't too happy about that."

"No, he made a big fuss. But when the driver threatened to call the police, he ran."

I shook my head. "Perv."

"There's always some drama on the bus. The last time I was leaving Vegas I sat next to this woman who was crying hysterically. When she finally stopped crying, she told me that she had driven from Pasadena but had lost all her money and her car at one of the casinos. The casino had bought her the bus ticket back. I thought, for as much money as they made off her, they could have at least sprung for an airplane ticket."

"How many times have you taken this bus?"

"This is my third time, round-trip. My father is on the air force base in Boise, Idaho."

"He's a pilot?"

"No. I wish. Then maybe I could fly up. He's a helicopter mechanic."

"That's cool," I said.

"I don't see him very much. My parents divorced five years ago. At first my father was stationed in Germany, then three years ago they transferred him to Idaho. That's when I started taking the bus to see him."

I thought it was strange. I was taking a bus to get *away* from my father.

"How about you? Why are you going to California?"

"I'm running away from home."

"Oh," she said, suddenly looking concerned. "Things aren't good at home?"

"No. My father's abusive. At least he was, until I finally beat him up."

"Wow. So he made you leave?"

"No. That was my choice."

"I'm sorry," she said. "I'd leave too. My father's really cool. I wish I could live with him."

"Why don't you?"

"We've talked about it. But it's hard with him getting transferred all the time. I might someday." She pulled up her treat bag and held it out to me. "You should try one of my chocolate chip cookies. I baked them."

I took a cookie out of the bag and took a bite. It was delicious. "You made these?"

"Yeah. I like to bake."

"They're really good."

"Thank you. Have more."

I reached into the bag and grabbed two more. "How much farther is it to Los Angeles from here?"

"About seven hours. We arrive a little after eight." She leaned back. "We better get some sleep."

"Good idea," I said. I stowed the cookies in my pack, then leaned back against the window. I woke a few hours later when the bus made a short stop in Barstow. Monica had her head resting on my shoulder. I liked that. I went back to sleep.

The next time I woke we were pulling into the Los Angeles station. The sun was bright and Monica was reading, holding an open Bible in her lap. She looked over and smiled at me. "Good morning."

"Morning," I said groggily. I looked out the window. The Greyhound station looked as sketchy as the one in Ogden except with more people who looked homeless. A lot more. The place was teeming with people. "Are we here?"

"Welcome to Los Angeles."

I glanced down at the Bible. Just seeing it made me uncomfortable. "You read that?"

"Yeah. Do you?"

"I used to."

She didn't ask why I'd stopped. Instead she shut the book, reached into her sack of goodies, and brought me out a cookie. "Here. Have some breakfast."

I took the cookie, even though I already had two more in my bag. I knew I'd need them for later. "Thank you."

"You're welcome."

I ate the cookie while we waited for the line of people ahead of us to get off the bus. We were the last two off.

Monica got her suitcases, then said to me, "It was really nice meeting you, Charles." She handed me a piece of paper. "That's my phone number. If you ever need anything, just call."

I took the paper, even though I had nothing to call her with. "Thank you. It was nice meeting you too. Thanks for all the food."

"You're welcome. So where do you go now?"

I glanced around. I had no idea where I was. "I guess I'll just walk around."

"Where are you staying?"

"I don't know. Maybe I'll just sleep on the beach. We're close to the beach, aren't we?"

Monica frowned. "The police won't let you sleep there. And it wouldn't be safe."

"I can always find someplace on the street."

Her frown deepened. "That's not a good way to start a

new life. There are people on the street . . . predators. And gangs."

"Like the Sureños."

"How do you know about the Sureños?" she asked.

"I just heard. I can handle myself."

"I'm not saying you can't, I'm just saying it's not a good way to start a new life."

I shrugged. "What else am I going to do?"

She hesitated a moment, then said, "Were you serious about doing yard work?"

"Yeah."

"Then I'll introduce you to my friend's brother." She paused. "I should probably warn you, though, his crew is all Mexican. Are you okay with that?"

Her question stung me. "That's no problem." I squinted. "Don't you like Mexicans?"

"Like half my friends are Mexicans. That's how I know that some people don't like them. Some people just have problems with anyone who's not the same race."

"I'm okay with Mexicans," I said.

"Good. Then I'll introduce you to Ryan. In the meantime, you can stay with me until you can find a place to live. Somewhere besides *outside*."

Her offer surprised me. "Will your mom be okay with that?"

"She'll be fine," she said. "You'll understand when you meet her. *If* you meet her. She probably won't even know you're there."

I had no idea what she was talking about.

Chapter Nineteen

*There is nothing simple about simple kindness.
Neither she nor I will ever know how much
suffering she has saved me from.*

—CHARLES JAMES'S DIARY

We each took one of Monica's bags and dragged them out to the parking strip at the south end of the station. I was exhausted from the ride and hungry, but the California air felt nice: it was warm and sweet, almost like it was perfumed. Ogden wasn't perfumed. If anything, it was the opposite.

"How are we getting to your house?" I asked.

"My friend's picking us up." She suddenly glanced over to an old yellow-and-white Volkswagen Beetle. "That's her right there. In the Bug."

As we approached, a young woman got out of the car. She was tan with short, dark hair. She was shorter than Monica but, like her, very pretty. The women hugged.

"How was Idaho?" she asked.

"It was good."

"Dad's good?"

"Dad's always good."

"But you're not moving there."

"No plans so far."

"Never," she said. "You're never leaving me." That's when she noticed me. "Who's this?"

"This is Charles," Monica said. "I met him on the bus." She turned to me. "This is my best friend, Carly."

"Nice to meet you," I said. Carly didn't reply.

"Charles wants to work with Ryan."

"That will make Ryan happy. He just fired two guys and he's had to fill in for them. He hates to work."

"Charles's father does landscaping," Monica said.

"That's a plus. Where are you from?"

"Ogden," I said.

"Ogden, Idaho?"

"No. It's in Utah."

"Never heard of it," she said, walking back to her car. "I went to Utah once. Hated it." Without stopping to breathe she said, "You can put one of the bags in the trunk. The other has to go in the back seat."

I was lugging the larger bag toward the back of the car when I heard her say, "He's pretty cute." A moment later she shouted at me. "Hey, Einstein. The trunk's in front. It's a Volkswagen."

I turned around to see her open the hood, revealing an empty space. My face warmed with embarrassment. I didn't know that VWs had their engines in back.

"Sorry," I said.

"Your pack might fit up here with it. But you'll have to

put the other bag in the backseat with you. Monica travels like a rock star. Big bags, small car."

Monica leaned in to me and said, "Sorry. Carly's a little *brusque* sometimes."

I didn't know what the word meant.

It wasn't easy getting Monica's bag into the backseat. Worse, it took more than half the space and I barely fit, squished between the bag and the side of the car.

Carly's Beetle smelled like incense, ketchup, and motor oil. (I have since learned that all old VWs smell like motor oil.) The car was dirty, filled with fast-food wrappers, paper Coke cups, and other trash. She pretty much used the backseat as a landfill, though the front wasn't a whole lot better. There was a plastic skeleton holding a rose hanging from her rearview mirror.

"I've got to get out of here," Carly said. "This place is so dodgy. When I pulled up, there was a guy peeing against that wall right there."

"Thank you for sharing that," Monica said, turning back toward me. "You okay back there?"

"I'm good."

"I can't even see you."

"It's tight."

"Where are we taking Sir Charles?" Carly asked.

"My place. He's going to stay with me for a while."

"How is Susan going to feel about a houseguest?"

"If she ever drops by sober, I'll ask. I bet it will be a week before she even knows I'm back."

⋯⇒◯⇐⋯

Culver City was only a little more than fifteen minutes from the Greyhound station. We pulled into a suburban neighborhood much nicer than mine back in Utah, though that's hardly difficult. Monica's house was small, a little dated but clean, and the yard was tidy.

"How long have you lived here?" I asked.

"Almost three years. It's my mom's boyfriend's place. He rents it to us."

Carly pulled into the driveway and turned off her car. "There you go, signed, sealed, and delivered."

"Thanks, Carly," Monica said. "I owe you."

"Do you ever."

"Want to get pizza tonight?"

"I've got a date. Marco."

"I thought you were dropping Marco," Monica said.

"I was going to, until he bought me a necklace."

"You are such a gold digger."

"Guilty," she replied. "I'm like a bird. I'm a sucker for shiny things. Speaking of boys, how come Josh boy didn't pick you up?"

"He's in Germany."

"He's always in Germany. When does he get back?"

"Next Wednesday."

"Then let's hang out while we can. You know how he is when he's around. He's like a human straitjacket."

"No, he's not."

"Denial ain't a river, baby," Carly said.

I wondered who Josh was.

Monica got out of the car, then pulled her seat forward so I could get out. Or at least breathe. I climbed out and pulled the bag out after me. Then I lifted the bag and my backpack from the trunk.

"Thank you," Monica said, as I set the second bag down.

"Yeah, thanks, Chuck," Carly said. "And welcome to California."

She backed out into the street without looking, causing an oncoming car to slam on its brakes. She drove off honking her horn.

"She's so weird," Monica said. She smiled at me. "Let's get you settled."

Chapter Twenty

The relationship between a patient and a counselor is a peculiar thing. I find myself wanting to act more sane to win her approval.

—CHARLES JAMES'S DIARY

Dr. Fordham's timer rang lightly. She reached over and turned it off. Turning back to me, she said, "Is this Monica the same Monica you were married to?"

I was surprised that she had made the connection. "Yes."

"And she's still in California?"

"Yes."

She nodded slowly, then said, "I think we should explore this some more. Thank you for sharing with me. You mentioned that you're leaving on some kind of an extended sales tour?"

"I'm launching a new product."

"When do you leave?"

"Next Tuesday. The third."

"Would you like to meet again before then?"

"Yes. Do you have an opening?"

"I'll make time. I'd like to continue on this while it's still fresh. I think it will help you."

"How about tomorrow?" I asked.

She looked at her phone and said, "I don't have anything available tomorrow. How about Saturday morning at ten?"

"You work Saturdays?"

"Sometimes."

"I'll take it. Thank you."

"You're welcome," she said, standing. I likewise stood. Near the door she said, "You're a very interesting man, Charles."

"Is that good?"

She smiled. "Usually. Though I've had some really interesting clients whom I wouldn't classify as good."

"Share one."

She looked a little guilty but said, "All right, but no names. My second year of practice I had a man who suffered from boanthropy."

"What's that?"

"It's a delusional disorder where a person believes they are a cow or an ox. He was kind of on the border, dreaming a lot about it. Then one day his wife called me and said he was in the backyard on his hands and knees grazing."

"Like King Nebuchadnezzer," I said. "Daniel four thirty-three."

"You definitely are an interesting man," she said. "In a good way. Now let's see if we can make you a happy one."

I grinned. "I don't know. What did Bones on *Star Trek* always say? 'Dammit, Jim, I'm a doctor, not a magician.'"

She laughed. "That's really funny."

I stopped at the door. "Hey, would you like to get a coffee sometime?"

Her expression immediately closed off. "Thank you. But I can't associate with my clients like that."

"Fraternizing with the enlisted men?" I said.

"Something like that."

"I understand."

"Thank you, though. That's very flattering."

"Don't mention it."

"I'll see you Saturday." She smiled. "And I'll bring coffee."

"Saturday," I said. "I look forward to it."

Chapter Twenty-One

The difference between winners and losers is that winners see a helpful incline to climb to the top where losers just see a mountain.

—CHARLES JAMES'S DIARY

FRIDAY, APRIL 29

I don't know what had possessed me to ask Christine out. Maybe it was because except with Monica I'd never shared such intimate details of my life. I mean, after that last session I felt like we should have shared a cigarette or something.

Friday morning I went into the office just to make sure that everything was ready to go. It wasn't. Amanda was waiting for me to arrive. She looked upset.

"Glenn needs to talk to you."

"About what?"

"Bad news. There was a miscommunication at the

printers. The boxes weren't printed today, which means they won't be shipped out until next Wednesday."

"My presentation is Wednesday."

"I know."

"We have two hundred and eighty thousand dollars in hall rental and advertising and you're telling me we have nothing to sell?"

"We don't have the new product to sell. We have everything else."

"I didn't spend over a quarter-million dollars to sell old product. Get Glenn."

"Yes, sir."

A moment later a sheepish-looking Glenn walked into my office. He appeared terrified. "So you've heard about the printer's screwup."

I crossed my arms at the chest. "No. I've heard about *your* screwup. I pay you to make sure that I have what I need when I need it. Will I have my Internet Gold packages when I need them?"

"No, sir."

"Wrong answer. And don't tell me who failed. *You* failed. And failure is *not* an option. Do you understand?"

"Yes, sir."

"So let me tell you how this is going to turn out. Unless you'd like to reimburse me the quarter-million dollars I've put out in promotion, I'm going to have six hundred boxes on the ground in Cincinnati by midnight, Tuesday, May third. Even if you have to hand-draw each package and drive it to Ohio yourself."

"Yes, sir."

"Tell Progressive Printing that if they value my million-plus dollars of annual business, they will call in a night shift, bump other clients, or get the owners down there to run the presses themselves—whatever they need to do to get our product for us.

"They're starting to take us for granted. Let them know in no uncertain terms that if my job's not done, we're done with them. They had the artwork with a week to spare. Their mistake is not my problem."

Glenn fidgeted. "And if they say no?"

"Then you will find a hungrier printer and offer them our million-dollar account if they pull this off. There are at least a thousand printers in America who would kill for that opportunity. All that stands between you and my boxes is your willingness to accept failure as a lifestyle. I don't care which way you go, but get it done. Do you understand?"

"Yes, sir."

"Text me when you've done your job."

"Yes, sir."

He just stood there looking at me.

"Get out of here, you've got work to do."

"Yes, sir."

He turned and ran out of my office.

Amanda walked in. "So?"

"He'll have my boxes. I don't care how he gets them, but he'll have them."

"I hope he can get it done."

"He will," I said. "He's got a baby on the way and an ornery wife. Maybe I should just call his wife."

Amanda smiled. "That's not a bad idea."

"If life has taught me anything, it's that there's always a back door."

"And if not?"

I looked at her. "Then we'll be interviewing for his replacement."

Chapter Twenty-Two

Without passion, we are doomed to mediocrity.

—CHARLES JAMES'S DIARY

SATURDAY, APRIL 30

I had the dream again. Only this time there were differences. First, the dream was more detailed and lucid than anything I'd experienced before. The flames were higher and closer. I could feel the heat more intensely, to the point that I groaned in pain. Fire was falling from the sky, bouncing off the road like flaming hail. I don't know why it didn't burn me up or hit me. There was one more thing. There were sirens this time. A lots of sirens. The screaming was louder.

I woke with my hands over my ears, drenched in sweat and shaking. I sat up and looked at my phone to see what time it was: 4:17 a.m. There was a text from Glenn.

Progressive Printers guarantees that you will have a
minimum of 600 Internet Gold packages in Cincinnati
by Tuesday night.

Funny how a little perspective can move mountains.
I'd never understood why people were so quick to accept
defeat. That's why I'm the boss and they're not.

I slept in, finally getting up at eight. I went to a window and opened it. The weather was cloudy but warm. I
changed into my exercise clothes, then went downstairs
to my gym and worked out on my elliptical for an hour.
Afterward I showered and dressed, drank a protein shake
with a raw egg and energy shot blended in, then drove
downtown to see my shrink.

❖═◉═❖

Dr. Fordham's office was quiet and mostly dark. We were
the only ones there. She was dressed comfortably in jeans
and baby-blue canvas tennis shoes. It was the first time I'd
seen her dressed down.

"It's casual Saturday," I said.

"I hope that's okay. I'm meeting a friend after our session."

"Of course. I'm grateful that you'd meet with me on a
Saturday."

"It's my pleasure," she said. "Come in."

I walked into the office ahead of her and sat in my
usual place on the right end of her couch. Dr. Fordham
sat in her chair.

"Oh, I brought you a coffee." She grabbed a paper coffee cup from her desk then rolled her chair over to me. "Here you are."

I took it. "Thank you."

"You're welcome," she said, as she rolled back to her desk. "So how are you?"

"I'm okay."

"Are you ready for your tour?"

I took a deep breath. "Physically I am, but emotionally . . ." I shook my head. "I'm a little worried."

"About what?"

"I'm having trouble getting the fire in my belly, you know?"

"You don't feel passionate about it," she said, restating my problem.

"No. I don't."

"Lack of passion sometimes occurs when our stated goals are incongruent with our inner desires. So the question is, do you believe in what you're doing?" As usual, she had zeroed right in on the heart of my problem.

"I believe in making money," I said. "And I believe in my ability to succeed."

"Then what do you think is the problem?"

I looked down for a moment, then back up into her eyes. "I don't want to hurt anyone."

"That's not a bad thing."

"It is in my business."

"Then maybe you're in the wrong kind of business."

I looked down again. "This is probably something we shouldn't tackle this close to my tour. The missiles are already launched."

"Of course," she said.

"So I had this experience I wanted to tell you about. Last Sunday I had dinner with an old colleague of mine. Actually, he was my mentor. He was the one who got me into the business. He told me to get out of it."

"How did you feel about that?"

"I was defensive. But part of me wondered if he was right. But then I felt like a quitter."

"It's not always wrong to quit. We should never hang on to a mistake just because we spent a lot of time making it."

"You're pretty wise," I said.

"Now and then," she replied. "So when we left off last time, you had just met your wife, Monica, on a bus. We were going to talk more about that."

I took a deep breath. "Let's see. After we arrived in Los Angeles, she invited me to stay with her for a few days."

"And did you?"

"It turned out to be a lot longer than that."

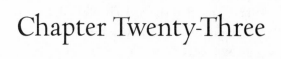

Chapter Twenty-Three

Monica has everything I want in a girl
except the absence of a rich boyfriend.

—CHARLES JAMES'S DIARY

SEVENTEEN YEARS EARLIER
Los Angeles, California

The evening I arrived in Los Angeles, Monica and I went for a walk around her neighborhood. Even though I'd never heard of Culver City before, the place was famous. The original MGM Studios, now Sony Pictures, was located in Culver City. Also Howard Hughes's aircraft company was here. A lot of movies were filmed there. They still are. I definitely wasn't in Ogden anymore.

Before we went home we stopped for dinner at a place called Signature Burger. Monica ordered for me their specialty, the Aloha—a large two-patty hamburger with a slice of pineapple. I'd never even heard of such a thing. It seemed like fine dining to me. On our way back to the house I asked her who Josh was.

"He's my boyfriend," she said.

It bothered me that she had a boyfriend. Deeply.

"How long have you been with him?"

"A couple of years."

"Where'd you meet?"

"At a party. After my parents divorced I went a little crazy and started partying a lot. I've read that sometimes happens when kids' parents separate. I'm not saying it's an excuse; it's a reason."

"I understand," I said.

"One night Carly and I went to this party at a friend of a friend's place. As the night went on, someone brought out acid. I had gotten drunk a few times and smoked weed, but I'd never used hard drugs. I had promised myself that was a line I wouldn't cross. But there was a lot of peer pressure. I was really scared but still about to do it when this older guy I'd never seen before came up and took my arm and said, 'Let's go.' He said he could tell that I didn't want to do it. Neither did he. He said that his work drug-tested and he made way too much money to go down that way. He was kind of my savior that night. He drove me to a pancake house and we talked to like three in the morning.

"It turned out that he's a military brat like me, except his dad has a high rank. He's, like, almost a general. He lived in Germany for his high school years, so he didn't have a lot of friends in L.A. We started hanging out. He's really smart. He speaks fluent German and has a really good job with a big German company. He makes a lot of money."

I turned to her. "Is that important to you?"

"That he makes a lot of money? No. But it's a lot better than being poor."

"Like me."

"Like us," she said.

When we got back to her street there was a brown Ford Ranger truck parked in her driveway. Its bed was crowded with lawn mowers and other landscaping implements.

"Looks like your yard guy is here," I said.

Monica laughed. "I'm the yard guy. You think I can afford to have someone mow my lawn? That's Ryan. Carly must have told him about you. He really is desperate."

As we walked up to the house, a tall, twentysomething man with light-brown hair and a receding hairline got out of the truck. I could see his resemblance to Carly.

"Hey, Ryan," Monica said.

"Money," he said. "You know how long I've been here waiting for you?"

Money?

"Then maybe you should have made an appointment," Monica threw back.

He walked toward us and we met at the center of the front lawn. "This the guy?" he asked, looking me over.

"I'm Charles," I said.

"Charles or Chuck?" Before I could answer he said, "Doesn't matter, I'll come up with a nickname for you anyway. How old are you?"

I fudged my age a bit. "Eighteen."

"Let me see your hands."

"Do you always say that when you first meet someone?" Monica asked.

"I'm a palm reader," he said.

"It's cool," I said. "I get it." I raised my hands. "You know, Jesse James used to ask the people he was robbing to show him their hands. If they had workingman's hands, he wouldn't rob them."

"I always knew I had outlaw blood in me."

"Charles really does," Monica said. "Jesse James was his great-great-great-grandfather."

"Really," Ryan said. "So judging from your hands, you work for a living."

"Yes, sir. My father does yard work. So do I."

He turned to Monica. "Did you hear that? He called me sir. I like that. No one in California has manners. You don't know any Spanish, do you?"

"Some," I said. "*Hablo español lo suficiente para sobrevivir. Comprendo más de lo que hablo.*"

"That's pretty good. High school Spanish?"

"Something like that," I said.

"So Monica told you that I'm hiring."

"Yes, sir."

"Can you start tomorrow?"

"I could start tonight."

"We're not working tonight. We start at five forty-five a.m. That a problem for you?"

"No. I always got up early to work."

"Good. It gets hot here. We start early so we can siesta during the heat of the day. Be waiting outside. Nothing makes the crew madder than waiting around for someone, and you don't want to start your first day on the wrong foot."

"I'll be ready. What's the pay?"

"Eleven dollars an hour."

I glanced at Monica then back at him. "Monica said you paid twelve."

"Monica's not signing the checks."

Monica crossed her arms at her chest and looked at him indignantly. He glanced at her and then breathed out. "All right. Let's see how you do."

"You won't be disappointed," I said.

"Good. I hate being disappointed. See you *mañana*."

He got back in his truck and drove away.

After he left, Monica said, "Sorry. Carly told me twelve."

"I'll get twelve," I said. "He calls you *Money*?"

"He has a nickname for everyone. He calls Carly Carl's Jr. It's just his thing. He'll have one for you." Her brow fell. "How do you speak such good Spanish?"

"My father's Mexican."

"Now I feel stupid about asking you if you mind working with Mexicans."

"Don't worry about it. I don't look Mexican."

"Your last name isn't Mexican."

"It was," I said. "It was Gonzales. I changed it to James. But I'm one-quarter Mexican."

"That's good."

"That I changed my name or that I'm Mexican?"

"The Mexican part," she said, turning back to the house. "We're having tacos for dinner tomorrow night."

I soon understood why Monica had said what she did about her mother. I didn't see her for the first week. In fact, I had pretty much forgotten that Monica's mother existed until one night when I woke at three in the morning to incoherent shouting and screaming.

I jumped out of bed thinking someone was attacking Monica. When I opened my door I could hear Monica's calm voice. "C'mon, Mom. Let's just go to bed."

I met her mother the next day after work. As I walked into the house, sweaty and grimy from the day, there was an older, attractive but worn-looking woman sitting at the kitchen table with a beer in front of her and smoking a cigarette. She screamed when she saw me. "Get out! Monica, call 911, there's an intruder!"

"I'm sorry," I said, backing out the door with my hands up. "Don't call the police."

"Mom, no," Monica said, running into the room. "That's Charles."

Her mother's eyes darted back and forth between Monica and me. "Who's Charles?"

"He's my friend. He's been staying here."

She examined me for a moment, took a drag on her cigarette, then said, "Is he paying rent?"

That's all she said about me living there. Ever. I discovered that the woman lived in her own world—one that barely included her own daughter.

Chapter Twenty-Four

It seems to me that there was a time when hard work was more prized than the clever avoidance of it.

—CHARLES JAMES'S DIARY

I liked working for Ryan, which is why I stayed with him for more than three years. After my first day at work he agreed to start me at twelve dollars an hour. After that, I really didn't see much of him. He managed things from his home, only appearing on the job now and then to inspect our work or to meet with one of our clients. After seven months, he made me the crew manager and I got a raise to eighteen dollars an hour and a truck to drive.

As promised, Ryan came up with a nickname for me. *Desperado.* Monica rolled her eyes when I told her, but I liked it. It fit my Jesse James persona. The rest of the crew liked it as well. It was all they called me. *El Desperado.*

Ryan had three crews. The seven-man crew I started with, then eventually ran, were all Mexican immigrants.

They lived together in a Compton studio apartment with a hot plate, a refrigerator they had salvaged from the home of a client, and a small black-and-white television. I didn't know you could still find black-and-white televisions. I never saw the inside of their place, Ryan just told me about it.

My coworkers' names were José Luis, Alejandro, Miguel, and Jorge. Two of the crew were undocumented immigrants: a second Miguel (who we called Miguel Jr. or "Miguel Dos") and Jesús.

They were all hardworking guys, but especially Miguel Jr. and Jesus, who sent almost all their income back to family in Mexico. I respected their familial loyalty but I would as soon burn my money as send it to my dad, though I did occasionally send money to my mom and Mike.

My first three months in California, I sent a postcard or letter home every week. Sometimes with money. For Mike's birthday, I sent him some expensive sneakers I'd never seen in Utah. I never heard back from him about whether they fit or not. In fact, they never once wrote me at all. Not even my mother. At first I made excuses for them, but, as time went on, the excuses didn't hold up. Eventually I assumed that they didn't care about me anymore and stopped writing. It hurt, but I had left them first. I guess I had it coming.

⊹⇒◈⇐⊹

The yards we cared for were in obscenely wealthy areas: Beverly Hills and Pacific Palisades. The homes were spectacularly landscaped with large palm trees, fountains, koi ponds, water features, roaming peacocks, hot tubs, and swimming pools. Technically, they weren't really homes, they were mansions. Or palaces. Many of them had more than one swimming pool. One even had a pool for their dog, a German shepherd named Goering.

One of the yards belonged to the TV star Adam West— the guy who played Batman in the sixties television series I watched reruns of as a kid. In my three years of working there, I saw Mr. West only once. I was edging the backyard when he walked out on the terraced brick patio in a white robe, drink in hand. I couldn't help but stare, a little surprised at how old he was but starstruck nonetheless. He looked at me, saluted, and then walked back into his house. He could have been Medusa, as I was as frozen as the statuary around me. That was the extent of my brush with greatness. I still tell people that I mowed Batman's lawn.

The next day I asked Ryan if I could ring the doorbell and ask Mr. West for an autograph and he said, "Only if you want to get fired." I never asked again. However, in my next paycheck envelope there was a scrawled note on Adam West's stationery that read,

Charles, keep up the good work. Adam West.

⋯⟶⟳⟵⋯

I suppose that it was during this time that my eyes were fully opened. I realized that there were different castes in America. People were divided not just by race but by money and fame. And while a person couldn't change their race, they could become rich and famous. This was a powerfully liberating concept—one could change his stars just by becoming one.

I became obsessed with the idea. Not just the wealth, but the fame and prestige. These people were more than rich, they were demigods—worshipped, feared, and obeyed. They were above the law. They acted badly because people expected it of them and responded to it. They were American royalty. I had finally found what I was looking for. I wanted what they had.

On the home front, things were going well with Monica and me until Josh got back. Considering my growing feelings for Monica, it wasn't surprising that I took an instant dislike to him. But I doubt I would have liked him anyway. He was as arrogant as a peacock and I'd had enough of arrogant pretty boys in Utah to last my whole life.

The first time I met Josh I had just gotten home from working overtime on a grueling, dirty job. My whole body, head included, was coated in sweat and dirt, and my arms were covered in scratches and dried blood. We had worked extra hours ripping out a thorny rose garden. Still, I was in a good mood because it was the weekend. I planned to clean up and then, with my overtime money, take Monica to dinner and a show. I never got the chance.

"You're home late," she said as I walked in. She looked me over. "What happened to you?"

"We had to tear out twenty yards of rosebushes. You should see Jorge. He looks like a mountain lion got him. He's ripped to shreds. Want to go out for dinner?"

"I'd love to, but I'm going out. I'm sorry, I forgot to tell you."

"Oh," I said. "With Carly?"

"No. With Josh. He's back in town." I didn't say anything, and she looked at me quizzically. "Are you okay?"

"I'm fine. I'm just tired. And hungry."

"Put a frozen burrito in the microwave. We've still got some of those bean and green chili ones you like."

Just then someone honked three times. Monica groaned. "Oh no, he's here. I'm not ready. Will you tell him to come in?"

Before I could answer, she turned and ran back to the bathroom. Then as I walked to the door, someone pounded on it. Not knocked, *pounded*. I opened it. Josh's hand was raised and about to hit the door again. He froze when he saw me.

I looked him over. He looked much older than me, even though Monica had told me he was only a few years older. He was slight of build and dressed in a stiff button-down shirt and tight, feminine slacks. Parked on the street behind him was a baby-blue Mercedes convertible with its top down.

"Who are you?" he asked.

"I'm the landscaper," I said. "Monica's not ready yet. She wanted me to tell you to come in and wait."

He shook his head, looking put out. "Women," he said beneath his breath.

I stepped away from the door as he stepped inside.

"So you're the yard guy?" he said.

"Not really." I put out my hand to shake. "I'm Charles."

He looked at my hand but didn't take it. "You're covered with dirt."

—
459

"Yeah. I work for a living."

He smirked. "I guess someone has to."

Just then Monica walked into the front room. Even though he hadn't seen her in several weeks, he greeted her with, "C'mon, we're going to be late for the concert."

"Sorry. I got off work late."

"Why? Someone croak?"

Monica glanced furtively at me as if she were embarrassed. "Good night, Charles."

"See you," I said.

Josh glanced at me but said nothing as he left the house.

"What a dirtbag," I said to myself.

I wrapped a couple of burritos in a paper towel and put them in the microwave, set it for three minutes, then went and showered. The water and dirt coming off me gathered at my feet like mud. The whole time I thought about Josh. *How can someone be shorter than you and still look down on you? Why am I so upset?*

Chapter Twenty-Five

To the narcissist, all the world's a stage, and everyone else is either a supporting actor or a stagehand.

—CHARLES JAMES'S DIARY

The Josh thing just got worse. He came by almost every day. He was always dismissive. After a week I asked Monica when Josh would be leaving again.

She gave me a funny look. "Why?"

"So we can do things."

"If you're lonely, give Carly a call."

"That wasn't what I had in mind," I said.

Josh rarely came up to the house anymore, at least when I was around. I don't know if I scared him or he just thought I was beneath him, but he went out of his way to avoid me. If I was out in the yard when he came, he would just walk past me without saying anything.

Still, even more disturbing than how he treated me was how he treated Monica. Their relationship was as one-sided as a pizza. Even with as little as I saw them together, it was obvious. Josh blamed Monica for everything, including his own junk—like if he forgot something, it was her fault for not reminding him. He talked about himself constantly and interrupted Monica if she talked about her own things. Basically he treated people like supporting actors in the Josh show. It was all I could do to not punch him out.

One night I decided to confront Monica about him. She had been out with him and didn't get in until after one. I was waiting on the couch as she walked in.

"Hey," I said.

She looked over at me. "You're still up?"

"Can we talk?"

"Of course. Don't you have work in the morning?"

"Yes. I needed to talk to you."

She suddenly looked concerned. She came over and sat down on the couch next to me. "What's wrong?"

"It's Josh."

"Yes?"

"I've been reading about people like him."

Her brow fell. "What do you mean, 'people like him'?"

"He's a narcissist."

"You don't even know what that means."

"Yeah, I do. And he fits the description perfectly."

"He's just confident."

"It's not confidence if he thinks he's better than everyone, it's narcissism."

"You're making too much of it."

"Does he ever ask you what you want to do?"

"Sometimes."

"What if you say something he doesn't want to do?"

She just looked at me. "He's not a narcissist. He just has a strong personality." She looked at me intensely. "You really stayed up this late to tell me this?"

"Yes."

"Why?"

"I want you to be happy."

"I *am* happy. I think maybe it's you who has the problem. Good night." She got up and walked to her room. I felt like my heart would break.

After that I never brought Josh up again. There was no point. But things changed for the worse between Monica and me. I didn't know how much longer I could take it. After three more weeks things were coming to a head. In part because Monica was gone all the time and I felt like a squatter in her house. But most of all, the jealousy was killing me. I'd never been so in love, so I'd never been so tormented. I couldn't stand seeing them together and I couldn't get her out of my head.

I finally faced the reality that the only way out of pain was through the front door. I had to leave. I told my yard crew, and Alejandro said I could move in with them for a while. Just another body, I guess. It wasn't the Ritz, it wasn't even the Best Western, but it would still be less painful than seeing them together.

I waited until Saturday night to tell her. As usual, Monica was going out with him. She always told me now. She was just trying to be helpful, but it always felt like she was rubbing salt in my heart's wound.

That evening she walked out in a low-cut sundress that perfectly accentuated the curves of her body. She looked achingly beautiful. She struck a pose.

"How do I look?"

I tried not to reveal how much she really affected me. "You look good."

She cocked her head to the side. "Just good?"

"Yeah. I mean, you look *really* good. Beautiful. Stunning."

"I'll take stunning," she said. "Josh bought this for me in Beverly Hills. He likes to show me off."

Check that box on the narcissist test. "Isn't it a little chilly for that?"

"Oh, you're right. I better get a sweater." She ran into the other room and came out wearing a sweater. We heard the familiar honk. "There he is."

"Why doesn't he come to the door?" I asked.

"It doesn't matter," she said. She kissed me on the cheek and walked to the door. "Have a good night."

"Yeah," I said. "Planning a big party. Probably a hundred women . . ."

"Have fun." She was gone. My heart ached.

After she left, I packed my things—there were considerably more than when I'd arrived—then drove to El Rancho and bought a large bottle of cream soda, some tortilla chips, refried beans, tomatoes, diced green chilies, and a block of cheddar cheese, then came back and made a huge plate of nachos.

I lay back on the couch and watched television. Try as I might, I couldn't get Monica off my mind. *What did she see in him? Why couldn't she see what a jerk he was?* I guess what I was really thinking was, *Why would she choose him over me?* It made me angry that I was poor and couldn't compete. Then it made me even more angry that I had to compete. Why couldn't she see that I loved her? Maybe she did. Maybe she just didn't love me.

It was almost two in the morning when Monica returned. I had dozed off but woke at the sound of the door opening. I sat up on the couch, rubbing my eyes.

"Oh, you scared me," she said. "Fall asleep on the couch?"

"Yeah."

She locked the door and walked into the front room. "What did you do tonight?"

"The usual party. A hundred women. At least. I kicked them out before you got back."

She grinned. "Thank you for cleaning up after."

"You're welcome. How was your night?"

"It was okay." As she started to pull off her sweater I caught a glimpse of a large bruise on her arm. She saw me looking at it and quickly turned away.

"You got a bruise," I said.

"It's nothing," she said softly. "I must have got it at work."

"You didn't have it when you left."

Monica looked at me anxiously. "It must have happened when I ran into the door at the restaurant."

"That's not from a door," I said. "I know bruises. That's from a fist." I walked over to her. "Let me see it."

She held her arm away from me, covering it with her sweater.

"Did Josh hit you?"

She didn't answer.

"Monica."

"Just on the arm. It's not like my face or anything."

Rage rose up inside me. "Why did he hit you?"

She turned away from me.

"Tell me."

When she looked back, her eyes were filled with tears. She wiped them and said, "He was mad that you're still here. He told me that I had to kick you out."

I was speechless. "What did you tell him?"

"I said no. That's when he hit me."

I stood up and got my keys.

"Where are you going?"

"I'm going to bash his face in."

"No. Don't do anything. It's not a big deal."

"It *is* a big deal."

"Please. Just let it be."

I turned to her angrily. I said, "I'm not going to be the cause of him hitting you. Either I confront him or I leave. Those are your options."

"If you leave me, you'll hurt me more than he did."

I wasn't sure what to say to that. Finally I said, "Two options." When she didn't speak, I started toward my room to get my bag.

"There's a third," she said.

I turned back.

"I could leave him."

I just looked at her. She looked frightened and vulnerable. Then she said, "If I left him, would you want me?"

It might have been the most beautiful thing I'd heard in my entire life.

"I've wanted you since I met you," I said. "Do you want me?"

She nodded. "Yes. So much."

"More than Josh."

"Yes."

I walked up to her, took her face in my hands, and for the first time pressed my lips against hers. It was the sweetest thing I'd ever felt. It was bliss. After we kissed for a while I said, "I was going to leave tonight. Seeing you with him . . . the jealousy was driving me crazy."

"Why didn't you just tell me?" she said.

"I tried. You didn't hear me."

"I'm sorry," she said. "I'm so sorry. I'll break it off with him tomorrow."

Chapter Twenty-Six

It is that to which we cling that drags us to the bottom of the abyss. There is real power in having nothing to lose.

—CHARLES JAMES'S DIARY

I should have known that there was no way that Josh would let Monica go easily. Narcissists don't give up easily. Failure is too much of an affront to their insecure psyches. Over the next two days he called and texted Monica repeatedly until she finally blocked his calls.

Early the next Saturday morning Josh got brave and came to the house. As usual, he pounded on the door. We were both still in bed. I got up and pulled on some shorts and walked out of my room. Monica was already standing outside the door to her room. "I think it's Josh."

"I'll take care of this," I said.

"Be careful," she said.

"Be careful of Josh? That's like worrying about a Care Bear." I walked over to the door and jerked it open, interrupting his assault on it and causing him to fall forward. It was the first time I'd seen him not all prettied up. He looked like he hadn't slept.

"Quit pounding on our door," I said.

"Where's Monica?"

"She doesn't want to talk to you."

"I don't care what she wants."

"I know. That's why she doesn't want to talk to you."

He looked at me as if sizing me up and then, to my surprise, he suddenly stepped forward as if to engage me.

"I see what's going on. The yard boy thinks he has a chance with Monica." He laughed. "If that's really what you're thinking, you're even stupider than I gave you credit for. Do you have any idea who I am and who I know? My father's a lieutenant colonel in the United States Army. He golfs with senators and congressmen. I work for Franz Krauss Deutsche, one of the largest manufacturing companies in the world. Do you have any idea how many people answer to me?"

"No idea," I said.

"More than a hundred. I hold their lives in my hands. While you . . ." He looked at me with disgust. "You're nothing. You're absolutely nothing. I could buy and sell you a hundred times over."

As I looked at him, a slow, sure smile spread over my face. "You're right. I am nothing. My father was an abusive drunk. I ran away from home at seventeen. I work with undocumented immigrants pulling weeds and mowing lawns and I drive a borrowed truck: I'm not important like you." I leaned forward. "It's just like you said, I'm absolutely nothing." I lowered my voice threateningly. "And that should really scare you. Because that means I have absolutely *nothing* to lose."

He suddenly swallowed.

"It's like my boys in the Sureños gang. They don't care if they're in or out of prison. It's the same violent life either way, except prison gives them free meals and a place to sleep. So before you threaten me, consider what exactly you're threatening. What do you think you're going to do to me? And then consider how much you have to lose, pretty boy."

He stood there, speechless. I noticed his knees were trembling. "I'm going to go . . . ," he said. He started stepping back.

"I didn't tell you you could go."

He froze.

"I'm not done talking." I stepped forward, narrowing the space between us. "Let me tell you how this works. Me and my buddies in the gang may be lowlifes, but even we know that you don't hit girls.

"You may have friends in high places, but they have to play by the rules or they fall. I have friends in low places. There are no rules. There's no place to fall at the bottom." I poked him in the chest. "Next time you want to harass Monica, next time you come to this house, you remember that. You remember that I'm no one and I have nothing to lose. Then you'll know why you should be very afraid."

He swallowed, too scared to move.

"Now run away, little man."

He took a few steps back and then, when he was out of my reach, said in the strongest trembling voice he could muster, "You think I want her? She's nothing to me. I've got girls all over the world. I was just using her."

"Get out of here," I said. I started walking toward him and he turned and ran to his car. He jumped in and sped off as fast as he could.

"Coward."

Monica walked up behind me. "What did you say?"

"Absolutely nothing."

I wasn't surprised that neither Monica nor I ever heard from him again.

Chapter Twenty-Seven

Monica is my pearl of great price.

—CHARLES JAMES'S DIARY

Life post-Josh was greatly improved. Monica and I got into a routine, almost like a married couple. Monica worked from ten to six at the Beverly Manor retirement home in Pasadena. I'd get home from work a couple of hours before she did, shower, and clean up. When she got home, we'd make dinner together, then go grocery shopping or watch television until about ten, when I went to bed. I always went to bed before she did because I had to get up so early. Also, with the physical nature of my work, I was always tired by bedtime.

Susan, Monica's mother, showed up only occasionally— usually when she and her boyfriend were in a fight, which happened like clockwork about every other week. She was usually drunk when she came. I don't think I ever saw her happy.

Still, at least she came by. I still hadn't heard from my

family even once since I'd left. I told myself it didn't matter, but it did. I couldn't understand how my mother could not care for me anymore.

One evening at dinner I asked Monica, "Why did your parents divorce? Was it because she drinks so much?"

"No. She didn't drink this much until after the divorce," she said. She looked up at me thoughtfully. "I guess it was a lot of things, but in the end it's always the same thing. They forgot they were each other's pearl."

"Their *pearl*?"

"It's in the Bible. A merchant was seeking pearls, and when he had found the one pearl of great price, he went and sold all he had to buy it."

"Matthew thirteen forty-five and forty-six," I said.

She looked a little surprised that I knew the verse. "So you know what I mean. When you've found the one, you cherish them so much you're willing to give up everyone and everything else to love them."

"The pearl," I said.

"The pearl."

"You're my pearl," I said. "You always will be."

"And you're mine."

Those were the best of days. I heard someone call seasons of joy "halcyon days"—kind of an endless summer. Even though my day job was exhausting, I was the most peaceful and happy I'd ever been. There was no one who wanted to hurt or control me. Even my boss was reasonably democratic. Most of all, I was in love, which was magical all in itself. There couldn't have been anyone better to navigate the currents of love with than Monica. She was beautiful inside and out.

And I was driven. As I daily worked the yards of the rich and famous, my ambition continued to grow.

-+-═○═══+-

I once read that it takes two things to be happy. Someone to love and something to live for. I had both those things—a beautiful woman who loved me and a dream of success that obsessed me. I was too young then to realize that, in my case, those two things were on a collision course. In the end only one of them would survive.

Chapter Twenty-Eight

Nothing drives us like hunger.

—CHARLES JAMES'S DIARY

I had been in California a little more than three years when I turned twenty-one. The night of my birthday, Monica and I discussed marriage. Marriage and family. She wanted a family. Maybe it was because she was an only child but she wanted a big family. She dreamed of having five children.

It wasn't the first time we'd discussed marriage. It was just the most serious discussion we'd had up to that time. In spite of our youth, she was for it. I wasn't sure. I wasn't against it, I was just indifferent. I didn't see the urgency or even the need, as to me it was just a formality. We already acted the part. We loved each other. We were exclusive. We were already playing house. And neither of us were earning enough to take care of a family. Especially a large one. As usual, nothing was resolved.

Still, I knew things couldn't go on this way forever. If

life had taught me anything it was that nothing stays the same. Susan was now talking about marrying her boyfriend. If she did he'd probably sell the house, meaning we'd have rent to pay somewhere else. Without paying rent, Monica and I had managed to build a significant nest egg of more than fifteen thousand dollars. I was a stickler about saving. I knew I wouldn't be doing landscaping my whole life—if for no other reason than to not be my father—but I needed work. And until the right opportunity presented itself, I wasn't going to jump. That opportunity came just a month after my twenty-first birthday.

It was siesta time at work. I was lying back drinking a cold pineapple Jarritos when Alejandro, the most ambitious and longest-surviving member of my crew, sat down next to me.

"Hey, Desperado. You want to go with me to a seminar tonight?"

"What kind of seminar?"

"It's the Master Wealth seminar." He looked at me seriously. "I'm not going to be cutting rich people's lawns forever. Someday someone will be cutting mine."

"Amen," I said. "How much is it?"

"It's free."

I looked at him skeptically. "Nothing's free."

"It's free to get in. But then they sell packages and books, things you have to pay for. Like real estate coaching, stuff like that."

"What happens if you don't buy anything?"

"Nothing."

I thought it over. "Yeah, I'll go with you. What time?"

"It starts at nine. We should leave at eight. It's going to be crowded."

"I won't be late."

⋆⇒◉⇐⋆

The Master Wealth seminar was held in the grand ballroom at the LAX Marriott. Alejandro and I walked in to heart-pounding loud music. The room was full of people, more than five hundred I guessed, most of them nicely dressed in business attire. There was more energy there than at a discotheque. I had never experienced anything like it before and was easily swept up into it. The place looked, to me, like success.

The event was a combination of religious revival, political rally, and self-improvement seminar all channeled to one objective, ostensibly to make us all unspeakably rich for the good of the planet.

The presenter that night was a man I'd never heard of before but seemed to be well known by the audience: McKay Benson. I was taken with him immediately. He was a tall, charismatic, fiftyish man dressed immaculately in a dark-blue suit with a crisp, starched white shirt and bright-red silk tie with a matching handkerchief peeking from his breast pocket. He had thick salt-and-pepper hair and a voice that rose and fell in timbre like an old-time evangelist's.

He controlled the stage like a master, keeping the audience engaged and mesmerized, as much with his delivery as with his message. He told us how, as a fourteen-year-old, he was left to care for his mother and two siblings when his father abandoned the family. He shared the story with such pathos that many around me, women and men, were crying.

"There's an ancient Chinese saying," he said. "When the student is ready, the teacher will appear. I was ready. I was hungry." He looked out over the audience. "Is anyone else out there hungry?"

"Yes!" everyone shouted.

"Are you sure?"

The room echoed with a still louder response. "Yes!"

"Starving!" a man next to me shouted.

"That's right where I was," McKay said. "I was hungry and ready and the teacher appeared—someone I never expected. A kindly multimillionaire who taught me the secrets to wealth. Who here wants to know those secrets? The secrets that made me the multimillionaire I am today!"

The room roared.

"As much as I'd like to, I don't have time to sit down with each one of you and teach you. It took me months to learn these secrets and years to perfect them. And besides," he said, grinning, "you couldn't afford my one-on-one time. But what you *can* afford is the supercharged Wealth Master course I've created to teach you those timeless principles of wealth."

He crouched down at the edge of the stage to speak to someone far from where I sat. I could only see the back of the man's head.

"You there. Yes, you. Let me ask you a question. If

there were a safe right here on this stage, with a million dollars inside, what would you pay for the combination?" McKay held the microphone out to the guy. "Speak into the mic, please."

"Whatever you want," the man answered. Everyone laughed.

"Wrong answer," McKay said. "The correct answer is, 'As little as you'll take to give it to me.'" He stood. "That's what I've done for you. The millions are there waiting for you. I alone hold the combination. So the question is, How little can I charge you?"

"You're probably thinking somewhere in the neighborhood of fifty thousand. It would be worth it, right? Fifty thousand to get a million dollars? You'd be a fool to not jump on that. But I'm not asking for fifty thousand. I'm not asking for twenty-five thousand. I'm not even asking for ten thousand.

"Now, some of you might be wondering why I would be willing to let this information, the combination to the safe, go for so little. Lest you discount the value of my gift, I'll tell you why." His voice softened with sincerity. "Twenty years ago I made a promise to my teacher—that dying millionaire who taught me these lessons. He said, 'McKay, all I ask in return is that once you get to the top, promise me that you'll throw the ladder back down for those still down below. Just like I did.'"

McKay looked at the audience with the tenderness of a loving father. "So that's what I'm doing right now. I'm throwing down that ladder. It's my gift. My offering. Are you going to take it? Or are you going to just keep living the same desperation you have for your whole life? You know what they say about insanity? Insanity is doing the same thing over and over, expecting a different result. Is that you? Or are you ready to take the ladder?"

"Throw us the ladder," someone shouted.

"Take my money already!" came another voice.

McKay laughed. "Smart," he said. "Smart. I thought you looked smart when I walked in tonight." He looked down at his microphone for a moment, then slowly looked back up. "How many of you are ready to name it and claim it!"

The crowd roared their approval.

"Repeat after me," McKay said. "Name it and claim it!"

"Name it and claim it!" they shouted.

"Stand up now and shout it. Name it and claim it!"

"Name it and claim it!" came the echo.

McKay grinned. "All right. All right. You got it. You got it. I knew you were smart."

Honestly, I had come to the seminar curious but skeptical—I think that was true of many in the room—but I had never before experienced the power of group persuasion. It would be years before I would fully understand how well planned and scientific the pitch I was hearing was, how expertly we were being manipulated and maneuvered. Before long I was on my feet shouting with the crowd.

"I'll tell you what I'll do," McKay said, sounding remarkably magnanimous. "Up here, in this corner of the hall, I have reserved exactly one hundred chairs for VIPs. Just one hundred of you. No, don't go yet. In just one minute I'll tell you how you can be one of the lucky ones in these chairs."

He walked to the other side of the stage. "How much is the ladder I'm offering? You know what it's worth. It's a bargain at almost any price. But today, it's just four thousand, nine hundred ninety-five dollars." All around me people started to stand. "Hold on, not yet. I'm not through. Like I said, it's just four thousand, nine hundred ninety-five dollars. But for the first one hundred VIPs in these chairs, I will sell the ladder for just nineteen hundred ninety-five—that's a three-thousand-dollar savings! You may now take the chairs."

People didn't walk to the VIP chairs, they stampeded. Two professional-looking people collided in the aisle next to me and were sent sprawling on the floor. People who weren't fast enough to get the chairs threw their wallets and credit cards on stage. They couldn't give their money to this man fast enough. I did the math—one hundred chairs, two thousand each. Two hundred thousand dollars in an hour. Incredible.

For the second time in my life I was truly starstruck. More than that, I felt I had finally found the path to my dream. This is what I had been waiting for. If I wanted to be rich and famous, this was a man who knew the way. I didn't care about the information for wealth he was selling, I wanted what he was demonstrating. I wanted to learn how he handled people the way he did. Best of all, this man had made it on his own. His childhood was like mine, and still he made it. McKay Benson was my new role model.

Alejandro was less impressed. "Man, it's nineteen hundred ninety-five for the starter kit. They want three thousand dollars for their Premier Wealth Package. If I had three thousand dollars, I wouldn't need their frickin' wealth package. Let's get out of here, bro."

"I'm not leaving yet," I said. "I have to meet this guy."

"Why?"

I looked at him seriously. "Because the dude is magic."

⋅⟶═◉═⟵⋅

An hour later, after the mob had lightened some, I approached McKay. Before I got to him he turned to me, his eyes blazing with energy. "What do you need, son?"

The question itself was powerful, throwing me off balance. "You were amazing. You are the greatest salesman in the world."

"Thank you."

"How did you do that?"

"What do you mean by *that*?"

"What you did from the stage. People were throwing credit cards. It was like . . . sorcery. I want to learn to do what you do."

He looked both surprised and pleased. Then he raised his hands and turned back to speak to the small group that still surrounded him. "God asked King Solomon if he wanted wealth or wisdom. Solomon chose wisdom and the wealth came on its own. We have a Solomon here today."

"Is it something you were born with?" I asked. "Or can it be learned?"

"A very wise question," he said. "When I started doing this, I couldn't sell a cup of ice water to a thirsty millionaire crawling through Death Valley. Then I read a book that changed everything."

"What book?"

"Now why would I tell you that? Would you ask the chairman of Coca-Cola for the recipe for Coke?"

"No, sir."

"Then don't ask me."

"I'll work for you for free."

"So I can train my future competition?"

"I could never be your competition," I said. "I would work for you."

"Until you don't," he said. "In the end, everyone's out for themselves."

"I'm different," I said. "I had a tough childhood like yours. My dad used to take me to the Dumpsters every Saturday morning so we could pick through them."

Something about what I said seemed to affect him. He looked at me with sudden interest. "What's your name?"

"Charles James."

"James like the author?"

"Like the outlaw," I said. "Jesse James was my great-great-great-grandfather."

McKay smiled. "That's good. You'll want to use that." He looked at me as if he had X-ray vision. "What are you currently doing with your life, Mr. James?"

"I do yard work in Beverly Hills. I plan to go to college next year."

"College," he said derisively. "College is for people who

can't think for themselves. What do you plan to study?" Before I could answer he said, "Never mind. It doesn't matter. Unless you're studying engineering or medicine, it's all a waste of time. So you have ambition, do you?"

"I always have," I said. "I want to learn what you do. I want to be like you."

He suddenly turned to the crowd. "Excuse me for a moment. I'll be right back." McKay put his hand on my shoulder and took me aside from the group. "Where do you live?"

"In Culver City."

"Where's that?"

"It's near downtown L.A."

He nodded. "Good. Over the next four weeks we have sixteen seminars in L.A. and Southern California. Can you make them?"

"Are they at night?"

"Wrong answer," he said.

"Yes," I said. "I can make them."

"Right answer. After my presentation, did you see my people walking through the crowd collecting contracts?"

"Yes, sir."

"They're called contract runners. That's what I want you to do. After each presentation, you go out and gather the sheep and take their credit cards. That's how it works. From the moment I leave the stage every second delayed makes them less likely to open their wallets. It takes a confident and enthusiastic personality to be a contract runner. Can you do that?"

"Yes, sir."

"Very good."

"Does it pay?"

His eyebrows rose. "I thought you said you wanted to work for free. Did I hear you wrong?"

"No, sir."

"Then I'd be a fool to pay you, wouldn't I?"

"Yes, sir."

"Does college pay?"

"No, sir. It costs."

"See, you're already learning. Be glad that I'm not charging you to work for me. Now *I* need to get back to working. I'll see you at the next seminar." He turned back to his eager crowd.

I went home that night a changed man. It was my epiphany, my Mount of Transfiguration. That night I told Monica that I knew what I wanted to do for the rest of my life.

Chapter Twenty-Nine

For hundreds of years, people have unsuccessfully practiced alchemy, seeking to turn lead into gold. They were just using the wrong gray matter as a base.

—CHARLES JAMES'S DIARY

I spent the next four weeks following McKay as he toured Southern California. I still worked my day job but four evenings a week, after work, I went home and cleaned up and then, even before Monica got home, drove off to the next seminar, driving as far south as San Diego and Oceanside.

Even though it was McKay's show, there were other presenters, each hawking a different product. I took notes during each of the presentations, studying the presenters' styles and pitches. Not surprisingly, McKay was by far the best of them all and the crowd favorite.

Then, as the presentations began to wind up, I'd check in with McKay's staff and help them collect contracts and credit cards.

Everywhere McKay went, people responded the same. It didn't matter their race, gender, or education. I've heard critics say that he preyed on the uneducated, but that wasn't the case—in fact the opposite seemed to be true. The more educated the people were, the more likely they were to lay down their money. McKay had created the ultimate business model. It's like he just turned on a faucet and money poured out.

Even though I was exhausted from my double work life, I was hooked. When it was time for the Master Wealth seminars to move out of California, I had to find a way to stay with them, which would mean that I'd have to quit my job.

I went to McKay to explain my situation. I hadn't even finished when he said, "I like you, James. You've proven yourself. I'll bring you on full-time. Go find Claudia and get your W-four."

I couldn't wait to tell Monica when I got home. She was brushing her teeth at the bathroom sink.

"I did it. I've been offered a paid position with the Master Wealth seminars."

"Congratulations," she said. "How much does it pay?"

"It's mostly commission at first. But they give me a daily stipend of fifty bucks and an extra fifty dollars a show plus two percent commissions on all contracts I bring in. One of the guys there is making more than ten thousand a month."

"Ten thousand a month?" she said. "What do you sell?"

"Dreams."

She rinsed out her mouth and then said, "What do you mean?"

"We sell educational packages that teach people how to be rich. McKay has a whole line of DVD and CD packages with workbooks that go with his seminar. They run from two to ten thousand dollars."

She turned to me. "You'd have to be rich to afford that."

"Most people just take out loans."

"That sounds risky."

"Life is risky," I said. "And you don't make money without spending a little."

"Did they teach you to say that?"

"Yeah. Did I sound stupid?"

"No. You were pretty convincing. When do you start?"

"Next Monday. We have a show in San Francisco, then we head up to Seattle, Spokane, and Portland."

She looked stunned. "You're traveling out of state with them?"

"Of course. All the shows are on the road."

"How long will you be gone?"

"Three weeks at a time, give or take a few days."

Monica looked at me as if I'd just told her that her father had died.

"What's wrong?" I asked.

"We've never been apart that long. I've liked how we've been."

I put my arms around her. "Me too. But I won't be gone long. And this is the answer to our dreams."

She kissed me. "Not mine," she said, looking into my eyes. "I already have mine."

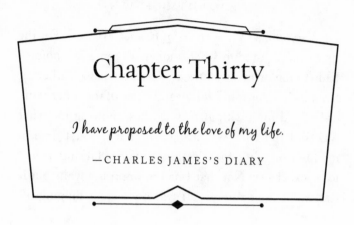

Chapter Thirty

I have proposed to the love of my life.

—CHARLES JAMES'S DIARY

As much as I missed Monica, it was exciting to be on the road with the show and the rest of the crew. I rose quickly up the Master Wealth ranks. Within three months I was their number two salesman. Two months later I was number one—an achievement that earned me a thousand-dollar-a-week bonus. I was making bank. I made more in one month than my father sometimes made in a year.

For the first time in my life I discovered the invisible gifts of my horrific childhood. Spending Saturday mornings in Dumpsters gave me an ineradicable hunger for success that sheer ego or ambition could never provide. Life had backed me into a corner and forced me to fight. It made me different from the other salespeople. For me success wasn't about ego or prestige, it was life or death. It was the fear of going back to where I came from. Success was keeping out of the Dumpster.

Also new were the fruits of financial success. For the first time in my life I had money. When I left home I hadn't even owned a suitcase. Now I owned a leather set from Louis Vuitton. McKay and a few of the other staffers helped me pick out new clothes, showing me what was cool and what was in fashion. For the first time in my life I bought expensive brand-name clothing. It had to be expensive. Not that I had to impress anyone but it was cathartic, I suppose. It was my way of flipping off the past.

Just six months after I started, I pulled into the driveway in a soft-gold convertible BMW 320. I walked into the house. "Monica!"

She came running out of the bedroom. "You're home!" She threw her arms around me. After we kissed she said, with her forehead still pressed against mine, "I thought you were going to be back this morning."

"I was. I just had some errands to run."

"I'm not your most important errand?" she asked.

"You're not an errand. You're my pearl."

She smiled and kissed me more. "I've missed you so much."

"I've missed you so much too," I said, stepping back from her. "And I have a surprise for you."

"What?"

"If I told you, it wouldn't be a surprise. Close your eyes." She closed her eyes and I took her hand and led her out to the front porch. "Okay, you can open them."

She opened her eyes. For a moment she just stared in bewilderment. "Whose car is that?"

"It's yours."

"Mine?"

"Go see it."

"Omigosh!" she shouted. She practically bounded out to the driveway. After examining the car from all angles she said, "It's really mine?"

"Yes."

"It's too beautiful."

"Not as beautiful as you," I said. I handed her the keys. "Let's go for a drive."

She drove out of the neighborhood, then down Jefferson Boulevard to the Baldwin Hills overlook. Back home, she pulled into the driveway and turned off the car. "I've got to show this to Carly."

"You know she'll be jealous."

"Of course." She laughed. "That's why I want to show her." She leaned over and hugged me. "You're so, so good to me. I just wish you didn't have to be gone so much."

"It won't always be this way," I said.

"How can it not be?"

I couldn't answer her. Instead I said, "I still haven't told you the best part."

"There's more?"

"Yeah. You can quit your job."

Monica looked at me blankly. "Why would I do that?"

"Because you can. Why would you work when you don't have to?"

"I like what I do. I'm helping people. It gives me purpose. Besides, you're gone all the time. What would I do?"

"I don't know. What do rich wives do?"

"I wouldn't know. I've never been rich. And I'm not a wife."

I frowned. "We still haven't done anything about that yet?"

She held up her left hand and playfully examined her ring finger. "Nope. It's still bare."

"I must have overlooked that." I reached into my pocket and brought out a navy-blue velvet box. She looked at it, then up at me. "What did you do?"

"Errands," I said. "Open it."

She took the box from me and flipped open its lid. Inside was a white gold band with a large seawater pearl surrounded by small, marquise-cut diamonds. She gasped when she saw it. "I've never seen a ring like it."

"It's to always remind you that you're my pearl of great price."

Her eyes welled up with tears. "Charles."

"Will you marry me already?"

She again threw her arms around me. "Yes, yes, yes. A thousand times yes." After a moment she leaned back. "Put it on me."

I pulled the ring from the box and slid it onto her finger.

"It looks like a flower," Monica said. "The diamonds look like petals."

"The jeweler called the ring a pearl flower," I said. "It's a seawater pearl. The diamonds are a tenth of a carat each. There are twelve of them. One for each hour on the clock, which is how often I think of you."

"It's perfect," she said, hugging and kissing me. When we parted she said, "When should we get married?"

"We could drive down to the county building right now and get it done."

"I want a real wedding," she said. "But I know it will never happen the way I want. My mother will just get drunk. And she'll boycott the whole thing if my dad comes."

"Then why don't we just get married in Idaho so your father can be there. We can buy a plane ticket for Carly."

A broad smile crossed her face. "I would love that. What about your family?"

The question made me hurt a little. "We'll invite them," I said. "Boise's not that far from Ogden. Maybe they'll come."

"Of course they will. It's a big deal."

"I don't know," I said. "I don't think I'm part of their world anymore."

She looked at me sympathetically. "It's their loss. You are my entire world. And if we're all the family we have, then I'm a lucky girl."

I reached over and hugged her. "I love you."

"I love you with all my heart," she said, her mood changing back to excitement. "So when are we doing this?"

"How about December?" I said.

"Why December?"

"It's the only time of the year we don't do seminars."

Chapter Thirty-One

"As a dog returns to his vomit . . ." Proverbs 26:11.

—CHARLES JAMES'S DIARY

Seminar attendance always fell sharply during the holidays, so four years earlier McKay decided to lean in to the reality and just gave everyone the month off at half pay. Then he went to Vail, Colorado, to ski, coming back full force the first week in January when people were still holding to their new year/new life goals of prosperity.

Our final two shows of the season were in Salt Lake City and Denver. I finished the second day in Salt Lake at four o'clock, leaving me the rest of the evening free.

Salt Lake City was only thirty-eight miles south of Ogden, close enough to visit my family. Knowing that Utah was one of our stops, I had been thinking about going home for some time. Monica and I had sent my family a wedding invitation several weeks earlier, and we still hadn't heard back.

It wasn't the first time I'd been back in Utah since I'd

left. I suppose I hadn't visited them before because I didn't want to face the reality that I was dead to them. But now that I had accepted that reality, I didn't feel fear, just the pain of rejection. For better or worse, I needed finality. I needed to either fix the relationship or let it go forever.

I hoped to fix things. I had changed. I wanted my family back—two of them, at least. Mike would now be older than I was when I left. I wanted to see my mother. I wanted her to be proud of what I'd become. I suppose some part of me even wanted to see my father, but for a different reason. I wanted to show him how wrong he was about me—that I wasn't a loser.

I rented a Cadillac. The guy taking my order was a little surprised. He said he'd never rented a Cadillac to someone my age before. Maybe I was just trying to prove something, but my father had a love/hate relationship with Cadillacs. He loved the car and hated that he would never own one.

I rented the most expensive Cadillac they had and drove to Ogden.

⋆⟹◉⟸⋆

It was already starting to get dark as I drove into my old neighborhood. I felt strangely out of place, perhaps like a soldier returning to a battleground years after the war had ended.

My childhood home looked quiet and small. For all the pain associated with it, it now looked impotent. The ground was covered by six inches of snow, and tiny specks of snow played in the air.

My father's truck was parked up against the side of the

house, looking about the same as it had when I left. It had to be almost forty years old by now. It was covered with snow, windshield and all, with about a foot and a half of snow on the cab. If my father was home, he hadn't left the house for a while.

I parked the Caddy in front of the house, then trudged through the snow up the walkway to the front door. The porch light was still broken from when I was nine and I'd thrown a rock at it. My father had beaten me with the handle of a garden hoe for that one.

As I stood at the door, I wondered if I should knock. I checked the door handle. It wasn't locked, so I slowly opened the door and stepped inside. The front room was dark and cold and smelled of mold. Maybe it had always smelled of mold.

"Anyone home?"

No answer.

"Mom? Mike?"

"Who's here?" came my father's gruff voice.

Of course he was home. I walked to the door of my parents' room. My father was lying in bed. At least what was left of him. Like everything else around me, he looked old and small and impotent.

"Look what the cat dragged in," he said.

"Where's Mom?"

"Who knows where your mom is. She left."

"Where?"

"I don't know where. She don't talk to me."

"How long has she been gone?"

"Why should I answer you? It was your fault she left."

I didn't say anything.

"Few weeks after you left, she left. She blamed me for you leaving."

"What an injustice. You were such a good father."

He looked at me spitefully. "You're no better than me. We'll see what kind of father you are."

Being compared in any way to him infuriated me. I was now larger than him and twice as muscular. I wanted to beat him the way he used to beat me.

"You driving a Caddy now?"

I wondered how he knew that. "I am today."

"Look at you, wearing a fancy suit, driving a Caddy. You some big shot now? You come to tell me you better than me?"

"I came to tell you that I'm getting married."

This gave him pause. "Okay. You told me. You can go."

"How do I find Mom?"

"You're talking to the wrong man."

"You always were the wrong man. What are you doing in bed at this hour? Are you sick?"

He looked at me darkly, then with an evil smile pulled the sheet back. His right foot had been amputated. The leg looked grotesque. The sight of it made me sick to my stomach.

"What happened?"

"Diabetes. I had it all along. I give myself shots now. Don't do much good, though. Doctor says way things are going I'll be blind soon."

"How do you get by? Financially?"

"That's none of your business. Never was."

In spite of our past, I pitied him. "Do you need anything?"

He scowled. "You wanna know if I need something. I don't need nothing from you. You left, you stay gone. You're not welcome here, boy."

"I never was. Good-bye, Dad."

Before leaving the house I walked to my old room. I flipped on the light switch but without effect. The bulb was burned out. But I could still see things from the hallway light. It looked exactly the way I remembered it, except smaller.

The bed, what had been my bed, was covered with all the letters I'd written to Mike and Mom. Even the shoes I'd sent him with my first landscaping check were still in postal wrapping. No wonder my mother and brother had never answered my letters. They didn't even know where I was. I left the mail on the bed even though there were checks in there.

"There is no God but me," I said softly. I walked out of the house without saying anything else to my father.

"Stay away!" my father shouted after me through the closed front door.

I started up the Cadillac, revved the engine a few times, and then, for the second time in my life, left a world I hoped to never see again.

But something my father said followed me back. Something painful. "We'll see what kind of father you are."

Years later, those words came back to haunt me.

Chapter Thirty-Two

Walking through peaceful grounds years after the battle, the soldier can still hear the cannons.

—CHARLES JAMES'S DIARY

Before leaving Ogden I stopped at the house of Lois Gant, one of my mother's Avon clients and best friends. I could hear the slow shuffle of her walker as she came to the door, followed by the sound of her unchaining locks and turning the dead bolt. She slowly opened the door. Even though I'd been gone four years, she looked like she'd aged twenty. Or maybe I'd just forgotten how old she was.

"May I help you?" she asked.

"How are you, Mrs. Gant?"

She looked at me quizzically, as if unsure of who I was. Finally, she said, "I'm sorry, do I know you?"

"I'm Charles James."

Her expression didn't change. "I don't know any Jameses."

"I'm sorry. You would know me as Charles Gonzales. Fiona's son."

The old lady's eyes widened. "Oh my, Charles. Of course. It's been years. Come in. Come in." She pulled the door open.

I walked into the small house and shut the door behind me. It was like going back in time. I remembered the old oak hall tree and the framed picture hanging in the foyer of Jesus holding a lamb.

"Please, come sit down," she said.

"I'm sorry. I can't stay long. I need to get back to Salt Lake."

"Pity," she said. "I miss having company. So how's your mother doing?"

"That's why I came by. I haven't seen my mother since I left. I was hoping you knew where she was."

"I thought she went with you."

"No. She left after me. I don't know where. My father doesn't know where she is."

"'Course he doesn't know, the old sinner. She was always too good for him."

"I won't argue that. So you don't know where she is?"

"I'm sorry. I haven't heard a thing from her since she left."

"Thank you, anyway. Sorry to bother you."

"Oh please, you're no bother. It's nice having company. Can I get you a cookie?"

"No, thank you. I'm okay."

"You always had an Oreo when you came by. Sometimes you came by just to get an Oreo. I still have some in the cupboard. Lord knows I don't eat them. I just have them here for the kids when they come by. But you're the only one who ever did."

"Maybe just one," I said.

"All right." She hobbled off to the kitchen. She returned almost five minutes later holding a single Oreo cookie in a tissue. "There you go," she said.

I took the cookie. It looked old and stale. Since nothing else in her house seemed to have changed since I was last there, I wouldn't have been surprised if the cookie was from the same package as the last cookie she gave me.

"Thank you," I said. "And thank you for everything. You were always good to my mother."

"That's the way the Lord Jesus would have us be. You were good kids. But that father of yours is some kind of a sinner, God forgive him. I suppose we're all some kind of sinners. I hear he cut his foot off."

"I just saw him. They amputated it."

"Well, the Bible says if your right foot offends you, cut it off. Better than having your whole body cast into hell. I guess that's what God helped him with."

"Thank you," I said.

"Good luck finding your mama. Please give her my love."

"I will. And thanks again for the cookie."

"Anytime," she said. "Come back soon."

As I walked to the car, she locked the door behind me. I tossed the Oreo into a bush.

Chapter Thirty-Three

Walt Whitman wrote, "We were together. I forget the rest." I think that pretty much sums up the day.

—CHARLES JAMES'S DIARY

Monica and I were married on Friday, December 11, about forty miles south of Boise on the Mountain Home Air Force Base. The wedding was small and perfect in its own way. The ceremony was attended by Monica's dad; his girlfriend, Eileen; Carly and Ryan from California; and three of Monica's dad's coworkers from the base with their wives.

At the last moment Monica's mom called and said she was coming, but she never arrived. We never found out what happened. Monica never asked.

The only attendee from my side, other than my former boss, Ryan, was Steven Vey, McKay's inventory manager, and his wife, Taylor. I knew Steven but wasn't close to him. I figured he was there because he was the only one from McKay's company who was geographically convenient. He lived in Meridian, Idaho, about ten miles west of Boise. McKay apologized profusely for not being there but he had made commitments long before I had announced the wedding.

The wedding ceremony was held at the base recreation center and performed by the base chaplain, a Mormon high priest from Mountain Home, Idaho. Afterward we had our wedding dinner at her father's place.

Monica was unbelievably gorgeous. I guess the only part that was unbelievable was that she was mine. My feelings for her were akin to worship. She wore a strapless, champagne-colored satin wedding dress with lace appliqués (with miniature pearls, of course) and a chapel train.

Perhaps the only thing more memorable than her beauty were her vows. She looked me in the eyes and said, "I promise to give all of myself to you. I will spend the rest of my life making you happy. You will be my one pearl of great price."

"You will be mine," I said. "Forever."

⊷≡◉═⊷

We spent our wedding night at the Grove Hotel in downtown Boise, then flew out at noon the next day from the Boise airport to LAX and directly to Maui for our honeymoon. At McKay's recommendation we stayed at the Grand Wailea resort hotel.

While he hadn't made it to our wedding, McKay had generously paid for three nights of our stay and the Spa Terme, which he said would be a sin if we didn't put to use.

The hotel was as elite as he said it was. Actually, more so. I ran into basketball great Michael Jordan in the elevator, and the king of Saudi Arabia and his many wives had taken the entire floor above ours.

Even though I spent a lot of time in the yards of the wealthy, I had never before actually experienced such opulence and beauty. Still, the greatest beauty on the island was at my side. A part of me asked the same question over and over: How could this miracle have happened? How could a poor, Dumpster-foraging boy, grandson of an illegal immigrant, end up in a place like this with a girl like mine? Only in America, right? It almost made me think that God didn't hate me so much.

–≡®≡–

Monica and I returned home from Hawaii, tan and rested, just two days before Christmas. Carly had decorated a Christmas tree for us. It was the best Christmas of my life, but at that time, pretty much every day was the best in my life. I was deliriously happy.

For Christmas, Monica gave me a Mont Blanc pen, a shaving kit, and a coupon book that she made herself, promising all sorts of favors (some I could share with you, some not). I gave her some expensive perfume that the woman at the Rodeo Drive Chanel store raved about and a pearl necklace. If you somehow haven't noticed, the pearl had become a recurring theme in our life together.

By then I had already been in California for four winters, so I was accustomed to green Christmases. We were still on vacation and reluctant to let our honeymoon go, so we spent the week between Christmas and New Year's at a bed-and-breakfast in Napa Valley. I had never before felt such exquisite love. The new year held remarkable promise. I guess that's why they call it the honeymoon phase. When you're floating along in such a powerful current of nuptial bliss, it seems inconceivable that anything could ever go wrong. It was the calm before the tsunami.

Chapter Thirty-Four

They say that distance makes the heart grow
fonder. I say it makes the heart grow mold.

—CHARLES JAMES'S DIARY

We returned home for good the evening of January first. I guess "good" was relative. The next morning I received a call from work with my flight information. The gears of McKay's money machine had started turning again. Two days later I left L.A. for subzero weather in Minneapolis. I was woefully unprepared for the cold, so my first stop was at the Mall of America to buy a parka.

Notwithstanding the weather, it was good to see the crew again, especially McKay, who was in good humor and enthusiastic to get back to work. January is a time when people actively decide to weigh less and earn more, so our seminar attendance was always up and our sales percentages strong. That month I witnessed our first million-dollar day.

I called Monica every day. Actually, the first two weeks I called her six or seven times a day, sometimes just to hear her recorded voice on her voice mail. After the first week she asked me to stop calling so much. It hurt my feelings.

"Why?" I asked. "I miss you."

"I miss you too," she said. "The thing is, you're not going to be able to keep it up. Then you'll call me less and less. Then, one day, you'll forget to call."

"That would never happen," I said.

"It happens," she replied softly. "I've seen it. It's like taking a coal from a fire. After it's been gone for a while, it starts to turn black. To charcoal. I don't want to see that with you. I want us to always be excited about talking to each other."

"I understand," I said.

"Let's make a rule: just one phone call each night when we go to bed, and once during the day."

"What if something big happens?"

"Then we make an exception. It's not like I'm ever going to get mad because you called."

"What about text messages?"

"You know I hate texting. But whatever you want. Deal?"

I breathed out. "Deal."

"I love you, my desperado."

"I love you, my pearl."

✦◆✦

The third week of January I was in Omaha, Nebraska, having a late drink with McKay after a full day of presentations when he said to me, "I'm going to hate losing you on the sales floor."

My heart froze. "You're firing me?"

He smiled. "I think you're ready for the stage."

This was an even less expected turn. "Are you serious?"

"Serious as stage four cancer. You've always been heading for this. You're good-looking, you have ambition, you have natural stage presence, and you have the stories. Your Saturday morning Dumpster story is gold-plated. And the fact that you're the great-grandson of Jesse James—it's almost too good to be true."

"*Great-great*-great-grandson."

"Not important," he said. "Facts are an anchor; imagination gives us wings. In our world, if the facts get in the way, we rewrite them. We'll definitely want to play up your Jesse James connection—not all of it, of course, just the rebel, legend side. We don't want our clients to associate you with the Jesse James who robbed people."

"What will I sell?"

"We'll start you off with the home-flipping package."

"I've never flipped a home."

"Doesn't matter. You'll triple your income."

"I'll flip whatever you want," I said. "Even burgers."

"Of course this will mean you'll be on the road more. Will Monica be okay with that?"

"She won't be happy about it, but she'll understand. A man's gotta do what a man's gotta do."

McKay laughed and lifted his drink. "To what a man's gotta do."

-•=◎=•-

I called Monica around midnight my time. It was only ten in California. She had gone out to dinner with Carly, which I was glad for. I hated it when she was lonely. She screamed with excitement when I told her the news. She sounded so happy that I didn't have the heart to tell her about the being-away-from-home part.

The next day McKay helped me develop my first presentation. He didn't have to do as much as he thought he would, as I had been studying the presenters for months. McKay taught me a few secrets about group persuasion and mind control that I'd never share here.

The first time I presented was unremarkable. I didn't embarrass myself, but I certainly wasn't knocking anyone's socks off. Sales were fair. I was afraid of what McKay might say, but he just patted me on the back and said, "You're doing great. It takes time to build a Stradivarius."

Two days later I presented again, this time in Kansas City. My presentation went better—as did my sales, nearly doubling. My third presentation was comfortable, the fourth intoxicating. There's something extremely powerful about connecting with large crowds of people. Seasoned performers call it the stage-light mirage—when the audience's love begins to feel real. It was addictive. Looking back, I suppose that this is where things started to unravel. I began to need them needing me.

Monica was right about our phone calls home. I remember the first morning I woke up and realized that I hadn't called her the day before. I checked my phone. She had called me three times, then texted me a blue heart emoji, our code for missing each other. The pressure and rush of performing had taken me into a completely different world. Being in different time zones added to the problem of keeping in touch, but the truth is, my head had been turned. In more ways than one.

I didn't know that there was a rock star–like status to being a presenter—one that drew groupies. Women began to give me their phone numbers and hotel keys, and even followed me to my hotel room. Every now and then, when I'd been away from Monica too long, there would be one who actually tempted me. In those cases I ran—just like the biblical Joseph ran from Potiphar's wife.

I also started to encounter the backlash that came from some of the clients who failed with our programs. In my previous job taking contracts, no one outside of McKay and the sales manager cared what I did. But on stage, it was personal. I was the face of the organization. I was the one taking their money. And when people weren't happy, they blamed me.

I was in the Dayton, Ohio, Marriott coming out of my room when a man cornered me in the hallway. His biceps were nearly the size of my thighs and he wore a hunting knife on his belt.

His wife had purchased my program a few months earlier and tried, unsuccessfully, to get her money back. The man threatened to beat me up right there if she didn't get an immediate refund. I calmed him down some, then called the home office and authorized her refund. Seeing how easy it was to refund her money only fueled his anger.

"You people are crooks!" he shouted at me. He then

walked out into the hotel's crowded lobby and shouted, "Don't get suckered by these Master Wealth crooks. Hold on to your wallets and run."

The experience shook me. For the first time it also made me deeply question the ethics of what we were doing. I went back to my room and called McKay but he didn't answer. Later that night I found his assistant, Amanda.

"Do you know where McKay is?"

She nodded. "He's in the lounge."

"Is he with anyone?"

"No. He's just getting drunk."

"I need to talk to him."

She smiled wryly. "Good luck with that." She walked off.

A few minutes later I found him in the corner of the hotel lounge. He saw me as I entered and waved me over. "Hey, Desperado. *Qué pasa?*"

"I've been looking for you," I said.

"You found me. What's up?"

"I need to ask you something."

"Take a seat," he said.

I took out a Wet-Nap and wiped off the chair, then sat down across the table from him. Only when I was close could I smell how much alcohol was on his breath. He gestured to me with a half-full glass of Jack Daniel's. "Well? What do you want to ask?"

"How many of our clients actually succeed?"

McKay didn't hesitate with his response. "Not many. It's not our fault, of course. You can lead a horse to water but you can't make it swim. More than half the people don't even open the box after they get home."

"Do they ask for a refund?"

"Fewer than you would think. Eight point two seven percent."

It struck me that he knew the numbers so precisely. "Why so few?"

"Shame, mostly." He lifted his glass and took a drink, then set it down. "Same reason people buy gym memberships they never use. They don't want to admit to being the losers they are."

"So we refund eight percent of sales."

"Hell no. The final's much lower than that. We put a few obstacles in the way of their refund. The fine print. It's not hard to deter them. These are quitters we're dealing with. You put out a speed bump, and they see a wall. That's how losers roll. End of the day, we actually refund less than a half percent."

I looked at him in amazement. "Less than one percent get their money back?"

"I wish it were less," he said. "Those losers just waste our time. Losers lose. It's what they do. It's what they're good at." He took a drink again, this time not breaking eye contact. "Let me put it this way. Just because you went to college doesn't mean you'll get a job. It doesn't even mean you'll graduate. Less than half of those who start college finish. Less than ten percent ever use their degrees. But do you see them lined up for a refund?" It was a rhetorical question. I didn't know he was actually expecting me to answer. "Answer me. Do you?"

"No, sir."

"Our program can reveal their inner loser for a whole lot less than the average student loan." He laughed. "How's that for a sales pitch? Buy our package, we'll show you your inner loser."

I didn't laugh.

He leaned forward. "What's wrong? Sudden attack of conscience? You think that what we're doing is wrong? That it's psychologically manipulative?"

"I didn't say that."

"You did, just not in those words. Let me teach you something, James. The whole world is psychologically manipulative. You turn on the TV, it's there. Listen to the radio, it's hypnotizing you. It's on the freeways and Internet. You can't get away from it—a hundred million entities vying for that six inches of real estate in your skull.

"And it's not just Madison Avenue. Punk rappers start rambling about cop killing and cops start dying. It's the way of the world. Everyone's mind is for sale. Even yours. We're just a bit more transparent about it." He looked at me angrily. "If you have a problem with that, you're in the wrong business. We sell blue sky. We give people tools to succeed. For better or worse we show them their true self. If they're too dumb or too lazy to use what we give them, that's not our problem. Snatching defeat from the jaws of victory. Should we feel sorry for those fools?" He looked me in the eye. "Should we?"

"No, sir."

"*No, sir* is right." He studied me for a moment, then said, "Don't ever forget that. Because on stage, even losers can smell hesitancy like a hog smells truffles. At the end of the day, we're in the entertainment business just like the rest of them."

I had nothing to say. I just sat there. McKay's gaze remained on me until he suddenly laughed. "Man, you look morose. Lighten up. Have a drink."

"I'm okay," I said.

"No, I don't think so." He pushed his drink across the table to me. "Go on. Have a drink."

The idea of drinking from someone else's glass horrified me. I didn't even want to lift it.

"Drink," he said.

I lifted the glass and took a drink, then gave it back. I wiped my hands on my pants under the table while he finished his drink.

He pushed the glass aside and said, "Let me ask you something, James. Do you know what the most dangerous animal on the planet is?"

"No."

"Take a wild guess."

"I don't know. The great white shark?"

"*Homo sapiens.* We're the apex predator on this planet. We're the top of the food chain, the sovereigns of slaughter, the maestros of murder. It's us versus them, eat or be eaten. You're either the butcher or the cattle. No in-between. No gray space. No fuzzy, feel-good places."

He leaned forward until the smell of his breath repulsed me. "This world is no place for sentimentality. The lion doesn't mourn the antelope and it doesn't have the teeth to eat grass." A broad, haughty smile parted his lips. "You,

Mr. James, just like your great-great-great-grandfather, do not have the teeth for grass. Never forget that. Because in the end it's that, not compassion, not mercy, and especially not love, that's going to save you. It's knowing the true nature of humanity that's going to keep you out of Dumpsters."

Chapter Thirty-Five

*I thought I was chasing success, when all along
I've really just been running from failure.*

—CHARLES JAMES'S DIARY

The next day, the McKay Master Wealth show traveled to Cleveland, home of the Rock and Roll Hall of Fame. I only knew this because our announcer played repeatedly on that fact as he whipped the audience up into a state of frenzy. I had to pretend I was with them.

I had been up much of the night mulling over what McKay had said. I came to the conclusion that he was right. I wished he wasn't but from my experience I couldn't deny it. Monica and I were living better than either of us had before. Joining him was like being given a VIP pass to life, the four Cs—cars, cuisine, clothes, and, most of all, clout. I had lived almost all my life on the other side of that fence, surviving off the crumbs others dropped and didn't miss enough to claim. I had lived controlled and beaten and, most of all, afraid. Fear was my lifelong companion.

You can't live the world the way you think it should be lived: that's magical thinking. That would be like playing baseball and telling the umpire that the rules don't apply to you. It doesn't work that way. The world is a game with set rules and set umpires. Wisdom says to play with the rules you've been given. It's not my fault they are what they are. I didn't make the rules. I don't even have to condone them. But to deny them was foolishness and would do me harm. It was what it was. And I was done with Dumpsters and hand-me-downs and dented cans. I wasn't that helpless little boy anymore. It was time to turn my fear to ferocity. I was an apex predator.

After my presentation I passed McKay on the way from the stage. I nodded at him and he nodded back knowingly. Considering how much he'd had to drink the night before, I don't know how much he remembered from our conversation, but from his expression I knew that he remembered enough. He knew I had bought what he was selling. He knew the kin of Jesse James was also a fighter. Maybe even an outlaw.

From that moment on I immersed myself fully in the game. No regrets. Take no prisoners. The tour went on. Time went on. I lost track of what city I was in. I lost track of the days. I even lost track of how long I'd been gone from home. We were on a Southwest swing through Albuquerque, Santa Fe, Phoenix, and Tucson, then back home.

I was on fire. The tour was going well for everyone, but

especially for me. I was paid a 15 percent commission on the packages I sold, which meant that some days I made more than fifty thousand dollars.

McKay was right. I didn't have teeth for grass. Hunters hunt. And you can't do that at home.

Chapter Thirty-Six

*When the space shuttle reenters the earth's
atmosphere, it faces intense temperatures of more
than three thousand degrees. Lately,
that's what reentry feels like to me too.*

—CHARLES JAMES'S DIARY

Financially, at least, Monica's and my situation just got better and better. Three months after my promotion we moved from the rental in Culver City to an apartment complex in Arcadia, close to the arboretum. Our new place was a little smaller than the house, but it was much nicer. The apartment was new and the complex had a swimming pool and fitness center and peacocks freely roaming the area. And it had the added benefit of not having Monica's mother crashing in drunk at three in the morning every few weeks.

But house and finances are just two pieces of a marriage. We had plenty of everything except each other.

Before my promotion I was on the road for two weeks, home for one. Now I was gone for stretches as long as a month. It took a toll on our marriage. The longer I was gone, the more moody and irritable Monica was. Some days she wouldn't even answer the phone when I called.

Even coming home became difficult, requiring a re-entry period, as if we needed time to remember why we loved each other. Sometimes it would take several hours after I returned for her to even talk to me.

Such was a Friday night that I arrived home from Fort Wayne, Indiana. It was late, past ten, when Monica picked me up at the airport. I put my bag in the BMW's trunk, then climbed in. I leaned over to kiss her but she only looked forward, pulling out into traffic. She didn't speak to me. After about ten minutes I asked, "Did I do something wrong?"

She didn't answer.

"If I did something, I'm sorry. I didn't mean to hurt you."

She turned to me. "Maybe you should mean not to hurt me."

My defenses rose. "What does that mean?"

"I hate this. I hate our life. I hate you being gone all the time. I didn't marry you to be alone."

I didn't answer her for several minutes, and we drove along in silence. Finally I said, "I'm sorry. It's not always going to be like this."

"How is it not always going to be like this? It's like you work for the circus."

I laughed. "It feels like I work for the circus."

She didn't smile.

"Look, I'm sorry it's this way, but that's just life. I'm paying my dues. If I were in medical school, you'd never see me, right? If I was in the military, I'd be away for months at a time. And I make a lot more than if I were in the military. Hell, I make more than if I were a doctor."

She didn't speak the rest of the way back. When we got home she stormed out of the car and into the apartment. I walked in after her. "Please don't do this. We have so little time together."

"That's the point," she said.

I groaned. "Okay. Whatever."

She went directly to our bedroom, undressed, turned out the light, and got in bed. I took off my clothes and got in bed next to her. "Good night," I said. She didn't respond.

Even though we were inches apart, I might as well still have been in Fort Wayne. About half an hour later I could hear her crying.

"Monica, I love you."

"I know," she said softly. She rolled over. "I'm sorry. I just miss you, okay?"

"I miss you too. More than I can say."

"When are we going to start our family?"

"Soon," I said. "Real soon."

For a few minutes we just held each other. Then she said, "I was thinking, maybe I would quit my job."

"Really? I thought you loved it."

"I do. I was just thinking that, since we have the money,

and before we start having babies, maybe I could go back to school to become a nurse." She looked at me with soft eyes. "Or I could travel with you . . ."

"That would be awesome," I said.

A broad smile crossed her face. "You really think so?"

"Absolutely. You would make the best nurse. My mother was a nurse."

Her smile fell. She was quiet for a moment, then said, "Okay. I'll look into some programs." She rolled back over. I couldn't figure out what I had said wrong.

Looking back, I can't believe how clueless I really was.

⊰⊷◉⊶⊱

As lonely as we were, our life continued on that way for the next several years. My income continued to grow. When our apartment lease came up we moved from Arcadia, paying cash for a home in Santa Monica—one with lemon, avocado, and orange trees in the backyard.

Monica signed up for a nursing program—one of those affiliated with a college but not at one. School kept her busy. Now her work schedule kept us even further apart. As time passed, I frequently reflected on Monica's analogy about the hot coal. It was obvious that our coal wasn't as bright as it had been. It wasn't cold, but it was definitely cooling. I just couldn't figure out how to get it back into the fire.

I considered that maybe having a baby would be the answer, but now Monica was against it. "I don't want to be a single mother," she said. "It's too hard. For all of us."

I knew things couldn't go on this way forever. Finally, I

began to consider quitting my job. Our home was paid off, and we'd saved more than half a million dollars.

I guess the thing was, I really didn't want to quit. I didn't know it at the time but I'd become addicted to the applause of the crowd. What I wrestled with at night was whether I loved it more than my wife's love. Or my wife. I knew that was the real question.

The other thing I wrestled with was the fact that with all my success, I wasn't happier. If I was honest with myself, which I wasn't, I would've admitted that I was driven but lonely and unsatisfied. I'd never been happier than during that simple time when Monica and I had been one. And there was only one way that could happen again. I feared, if I waited much longer, it might be too late.

Without telling Monica or McKay, I began to plan my exit. Then something happened that changed everything.

Chapter Thirty-Seven

Just as I was about to change my seat on the train, the train changed tracks.

—CHARLES JAMES'S DIARY

I was in Montgomery, Alabama, when my life hit a major junction. Maybe it was appropriate that it happened there, as Montgomery is the kind of place where worlds change. During the Civil War it was the first capital of the Confederacy, and later it became the center of the civil rights movement as the home of Martin Luther King Jr.'s Baptist church and the Rosa Parks bus strike.

I like Montgomery. There's still an antiquity to the city, a southern formality and properness that, outside of Savannah, you don't find anyplace else. (Especially not 150 miles south in Mobile, where people still believe in leprechauns and throw MoonPies on the stage when they get excited. Prime territory for the McKay wealth machine.)

I had just finished a strong presentation to about six hundred attendees and was surrounded by a crowd of potential buyers near the sales tables, when I noticed a couple looking at me from a dozen yards off.

They weren't hard to notice. In fact, they looked out of place, as if someone was doing a fashion shoot in the middle of a crowded auditorium. They were beautiful people. The man was handsome and well-dressed in a trim, ash-gray suit that shimmered as if it were wet. His hair was perfectly coiffed and he wore pointed Italian shoes and a white silk shirt with black buttons and no tie. He looked more than fashionable, he looked rich.

Even more noticeable was the woman standing next to him. She was gorgeous—magazine Photoshopped gorgeous. It was evident that I wasn't the only one who thought so, as pretty much everyone who walked by her took a glance or two. She was younger than the man, probably close to my age, mid to late twenties, and only an inch shorter than him, though her height was aided by stiletto heels. She had a stunning figure—a narrow waist, perfectly accented by a low-cut, body-hugging dress. Her brunette hair was tightly pulled back from her forehead, and she had high cheekbones and exotic, almond-shaped eyes. *She should be a model*, I thought, *if she isn't one already.*

I made brief eye contact with the man, and he smiled at me confidently. There was an obvious air of authority about him.

As the crowd around me began to dwindle, the man, with the woman at his side, walked up to me. They stood a couple of yards off waiting patiently as a young college student rambled on about his financial ambitions. Finally I connected the student with one of the contract runners and turned to the couple. "What can I do for you?"

"You did a good job up there," the man said. "You owned the audience."

"Thank you. Do you have any questions about my real estate package?"

He smiled. "I don't need your product. I'm interested in you."

"Excuse me?"

"My name is Chris Folger. This is my assistant, Mila."

She was already smiling but slightly cocked her head. "Hello."

"Hi," I said.

Chris handed me a business card.

FOLGER MANAGEMENT GROUP

Chris Folger
CEO
Birmingham, Alabama • London, England

I looked up at him. "What can I do for you, Mr. Folger?"

"Not as much as I can do for you. This is the second time I've seen your performance. I was in Birmingham last night. You just keep getting better."

I looked at him curiously. I couldn't imagine why he would be following me.

"I think your greatest asset, besides your obvious charisma, is your ability to create an image in your listeners' minds. You're a master at telling a story. Ancestor of Jesse James is brilliant and the Dumpster story, I don't know if it's true or not, but it's genius. Truthfully, I'd be more impressed if neither story were true."

"They're both true," I said.

"Platinum," he said. "Do you mind me asking how old you are?"

"I'm twenty-five."

"You're young," the woman said.

"Twenty-five," he repeated. "And you're already better at this than your boss. If you don't mind me asking, what's your take? Seventeen, twenty percent? Or is it a graduated scale?"

"It's a flat fifteen," I said. I don't know what it was about him that made me willing to share such private information.

He nodded. "Not as high as it should be, but you're good at what you do, so I'm sure you're not hurting."

His comment bothered me. "What can I do for you, Mr. Folger?"

"Call me Chris," he said. "I'll be crassly direct. I like money, Mr. James. And judging from your presentation, I'm pretty sure you do too. I want to make even more money by helping you make more money than you ever believed possible. I'm talking *real* money. Miami beach house, private jet money, if you know what I mean." His voice lowered as if he were telling me a secret. I suppose he was. "How would you like to have your own branded seminars and not only make half on your sales but twenty-five percent of the show's take?"

I just looked at him. "Selling's the easy part. It's filling the seats that's the challenge."

"That's the easy part for me. That's what I do. Or my firm does. Among our holdings we have convention and presentation companies. We own two network marketing companies and two of the largest Comic Cons in the U.S. What we don't have is someone doing what you do. My partners and I want to change that and we think you're the man to do it. We're willing to invest serious money in you, Mr. James. In fact, I'm prepared to sign a million-dollar one-year guarantee to retain your services."

The offer stunned me.

"What do you think?"

I looked down. "I'm not sure."

He laughed incredulously. "Really? I just offered you a million dollars, and you're not sure?"

I looked at him, then over at Mila. She bit down on her lower lip.

"What would possibly keep you from working with me?" he asked.

"It's just . . . sudden. I work for McKay. He's my mentor."

Chris said to Mila, "Very nice. Loyalty. I like loyalty." He turned back to me. "As long as it's well placed. The student doesn't stay in college because he likes the professor. He moves on to do what he was meant to do. In this case, the student has surpassed the teacher."

Mila said, "You were the star up there today."

"Look at it this way," Chris said. "McKay Benson preaches the virtue of unlimited acquisition of wealth. Self-interest aside, he should be proud of you wanting more."

It was hard to argue with his logic.

"What you do is like being a sports star. Sometimes athletes get traded to a different team. It's nothing personal, it's just how the game works. We're starting a new team. You're a franchise player. Does that make sense?"

I nodded. "Yes."

"Good," he said. "Where do you go next?"

"Des Moines."

"Des Moines," he echoed. "Rivière des Moines—River of the Monks. The only place in the world where they eat fried peanut butter and jelly on a stick."

Mila grimaced. "What was that other thing they were eating? Chocolate-covered bacon on a stick?"

"If they can put it on a stick, safe bet they'll eat it," Chris said.

"I haven't had the pleasure," I said.

"Trust me, it's not," he replied. "When do you leave?"

"Tomorrow morning. But I'm not in a hurry. We have a three-day break between shows."

"Perfect. If you're interested in hearing my offer, I can drive you up to Birmingham and show you around our offices and let you meet my partners."

Mila leaned forward. "The Folger Group only does big deals, Mr. James. We think you're a big deal."

"Yes, we do," Chris said. "The question is, do you?"

I hesitated with my reply. "I should hope so."

Mila smiled. "I should hope so too."

"So, are you interested?"

I looked down at his card, around at the people I worked with, and back at him. "I'll have to change my flight."

He smiled. "Good. I'm glad to see you follow your own advice. I'll pick you up in the morning. Say nine?"

I shook my head. "That won't work. I'm having break-fast with McKay at eight thirty."

"What time is good for you, Mr. James?" Mila asked.

"McKay is leaving for the airport at around ten."

"How about I pick you up at ten forty-five?" Chris said.

"That would work. And when would I be back?"

"Birmingham is about ninety minutes from here."

"Sixty, the way you drive," Mila said lightly.

Chris smiled as he turned back to me. "When do you need to be back?"

"I need to see when I can rebook my flight out of here."

"There's no need to come back to Montgomery," Mila said. "It would be more convenient for you to fly out of Birmingham. It has more flights. Let me take care of you. I'll check on flights this afternoon. What time would you like to leave—tomorrow evening or Saturday morning?"

"Either works," I said. "When I get to Des Moines, I'm just going to be sitting in a hotel room."

Chris nodded. "That being the case, let's book your flight for Saturday, so if things go well, we can have dinner with some of my associates and start making plans. Mila, book Mr. James a suite at the Westin."

"Of course," she said, smiling at me. "Have you stayed there before?"

"I don't think so."

"You'll be very well taken care of. I guarantee it."

"Thank you."

"No, thank you for talking with us," Chris said. "There are exciting things ahead. For all of us."

"Bye-bye," Mila said.

The two of them walked off. A line from an Eagles song crossed my mind. *This could be heaven or this could be hell.*

Chapter Thirty-Eight

Lures must be shiny and desirable to hook their prey.

—CHARLES JAMES'S DIARY

The next morning McKay missed his wake-up call and probably would have missed his flight as well had his assistant, Amanda, not called to check on him. Out of necessity he canceled our breakfast, though he stopped by my room on his way out of the hotel.

"I just wanted to share some good news," he said. "You were the number one haul yesterday."

"That's great," I said. It was the first time I'd achieved that.

"Great? It's fantastic. You actually beat me. No one beats me." He slapped me on the shoulder. "I'm glad I decided to give that poor little Dumpster boy a chance. I'll see you in Des Moines."

"Travel safe," I said.

As I shut the door I was flooded by guilt. Either he

knew something was up or the universe was torment-
ing me.

⊷══◉═══⊷

At ten forty I carried my bag down to the lobby and
checked out of my hotel. Five minutes later Chris Folger
arrived to pick me up. He was alone in a charcoal-gray
Bentley—a half-million-dollar car. I only knew this because the tech guys backstage spent a good deal of down-
time talking about their dream cars and dream women.

The drive from Montgomery to Birmingham was only
about ninety miles, which we covered in less than sev-
enty minutes. Mila hadn't exaggerated about Chris liking
speed. Just outside Montgomery he accelerated to show
me what the Bentley could do. It actually threw me back
in my seat. I could feel the g-forces in my head.

"How do you like that?" he said, coasting back to an
almost legal speed. "That's what six hundred and forty
horsepower feels like."

"It feels like a jet fighter," I replied.

"Exactly."

As we drove, Chris asked me questions about my
childhood. He wondered how I could have come from
such a background and done so well.

"Hard things don't always make life harder," I said. "It
takes something hard to sharpen steel."

He glanced over at me. "Well said. You might want
to use that onstage." He looked back ahead. "So about
today. We're going to be meeting with my two partners
and Mila. You remember Mila."

233

"She's kind of hard to forget," I said.

"Yes, she is."

⋆═◉═⋆

We drove directly to Chris's private residence, a sixty-five-hundred-square-foot southern-architectural-style home built on three acres of property in the Abingdon section of Mountain Brook, one of Birmingham's most affluent suburbs. The yard was expertly manicured, something I was still in the habit of noticing and, with my OCD, listing in my mind what it would take to maintain.

Mature Japanese maples lined the front entrance next to concrete balustrades and brick archways. To the side of the house was a red clay tennis court and a swimming pool with statuary and fountains. Behind the pool was a pool house larger than my childhood home. It was smaller but every bit as nice as the places I used to care for in Beverly Hills.

Chris pulled his car into the garage and we walked inside. The home was open and spacious with marble floors and high vaulted ceilings.

Past the kitchen and dining room, seated on leather couches in front of a fireplace and an easel, were Mila and Chris's two partners. Both men looked to be in their mid-forties. One was very tall, easily six foot seven, tan with sandy hair, and wearing a golf shirt. The other was about my size; he wore a dress shirt and tie. He was muscular and dark-haired like me. They both stood as we entered. Only Mila remained seated.

"Gentlemen," Chris said, "this is Mr. James. Charles, these are my partners."

234

Both men enthusiastically greeted me, stretching out their hands as I reached them.

"I'm Kelly Birch," the tall man said. "It's nice to finally meet you."

"I'm Jeremy Cunningham," said the other.

I shook both of their hands. "Charles James. You can call me Charles."

Mila was sitting on the couch. She wore a leather skirt and a low-cut cream silk blouse. She waved with her fingers. "It's good to see you again."

"Likewise," I said.

"Let's begin. Please, sit right here," Chris said, gesturing to a plush, olive-green velvet armchair with button-tufted upholstery. The chair faced the easel. Everyone sat except for the tall man, Kelly, who walked to the easel.

"We're pleased that you were willing to entertain our proposal," he said. "We are very excited about this opportunity and think that, once you understand our vision, you will be as well. We believe that, working with you, we can create a company producing more than three hundred million dollars a year in revenue. This is the company." He lifted the sheet on the easel exposing a stylish logo:

CHARLES JAMES
WEALTH SEMINARS

"What do you think?" Chris asked.

"The logo font is the same used on the dollar," Jeremy said. "A little subliminal nudge."

Even though Chris had talked about the seminars

being mine, he hadn't told me what he planned on calling them. "You're naming the seminars after me?"

"Of course," Chris said. "You're the star."

"That's right," Kelly said. "You're the face of the machine. I believe Chris shared with you our level of commitment. We are willing to pay you a guaranteed base of a million dollars the first year backed with commissions. As well as thirty-percent stock in the company."

My heart was pounding, but I did my best to appear only marginally interested.

The other man, Jeremy, opened a briefcase and brought out some paperwork. "We've had our lawyers draft a contract." He handed it to me. It was thick, about twenty pages long. I cursorily thumbed through it.

"I'll have to run this by my attorney," I said, even though I didn't have one. "And my wife."

"Of course," Chris said. "We'd expect that."

I looked back down at the contract and began reading it more carefully. On the fifth page I read through something that stopped me. "What's this proprietary information clause?"

"Your value to our venture is more than just your presentation skills," Kelly said. "You also bring to the table industry expertise that you've garnered working alongside McKay Benson. We assume you know his plans for the year, his sales strategies, and how he operates his company profitably. The clause just says that you agree to share with our venture all knowledge you have in order to help us acquire as many of your former clients as we can."

I looked up at him. "By *acquire* you mean *steal*."

"You say that as if someone owns them," Jeremy said.

"It's business," Kelly said. "The very nature of this business is competition."

"Make no mistake," Jeremy said. "We play hardball."

Chris turned to me. "We don't mean to come across so Machiavellian. But in this world, McKay's not your friend anymore, he's your competition. If that's something you can't do, we should get this out on the table now. Because if you're not all in, neither are we."

I looked at the four of them, back down at the million-dollar contract in my hands, then back at them.

"No. I'm fine with it. Let's do this."

Chapter Thirty-Nine

The sirens of success have sharp teeth.

—CHARLES JAMES'S DIARY

"Before you boys get in any deeper," Mila said, "it's almost two o'clock. You should get some lunch."

"She's right," Chris said.

Mila turned to me. "Do you like sushi?"

"I love it."

She stood. "I'll get us a table at Jinsei," she said to Chris.

We drove to downtown Birmingham in two cars, Kelly and Jeremy in a Land Rover and Chris, Mila, and I in Chris's Bentley. Jinsei was a sushi bar with an authentic Japanese ambience—the kind of place where you take off your shoes and sit around a low table.

Chris and his partners didn't talk about their business proposal at lunch; rather, Kelly and Jeremy talked about other recent enterprises, which were myriad.

"Kelly was a basketball star at Auburn," Mila said.

Kelly shook his head. "I thought I was going to go pro until the second game of the NCAA tournament, when I blew out my knee. Torn ACL."

"I'm sorry," I said.

"I'm not. Best thing that ever happened to me. I'm loving life with these guys. And life as an athlete comes with an expiration date and no tomorrow. My potential here is unlimited. What we're doing here is empire building."

Chris lifted a glass of warm sake. "To new empires."

We all toasted.

After lunch we drove just a few miles to their office building, an independent three-story glass and brick structure situated in a lush business park of identical buildings. FOLGER MANAGEMENT GROUP was posted in twelve-inch-high letters across the front entry.

Even though it was Saturday, there were still people at work. The reception area was opulent and the room glowed a soft gold from the alabaster sconces and recessed lighting. The floors were white marble with black marble accent diamonds. A long Persian rug ran the length of the reception area to a polished redwood reception desk with a marble counter. Behind the desk was the company name in brass letters on aqua-blue glass. A crystal chandelier hung above the desk.

"Welcome to our humble abode," Chris said.

"Humble?" I replied.

Mila touched my arm. "We're a very *affluent* company."

Affluent. The word still reminded me of the time on the Greyhound bus when I first heard it from Monica.

Chris turned to face me. "I'm sorry to interrupt our meeting, but we have a few fires to put out. Mila, if you wouldn't mind giving Charles the nickel tour. We'll meet up in the conference room in thirty."

"I'd love to," she said, again touching my arm. "If you'll come with me."

Chris hadn't exaggerated the extent of their company's holdings. One floor was dedicated almost completely to real estate. They owned office buildings all across the South and Midwest. Mila told me that they had more than a billion dollars in assets under management.

Near their dining area there was a wall adorned with pictures of Chris and his partners with various celebrities: actors, musicians, and politicians.

After the tour, Mila led me to the glass-walled conference room on the main floor. Chris, Kelly, and Jeremy were already seated around a high-polish maple conference table surrounded by fourteen high-back leather chairs.

"Let's talk business," Chris said.

For the next four hours we strategized about how to build a billion-dollar business. The attention, wealth, and flattery were intoxicating, and the more excited I became about the venture, the more I found myself sharing some of McKay's most coveted trade secrets.

"You know who we really need," I said, leaning back, my fingers laced behind my head. "McKay's assistant, Amanda Glade. She knows more about the business than McKay does. She knows all the vendors, production schedules, event planners, media, everything. We used to joke that if she ever wanted the company, all she needed to do was give McKay a document to sign that gave her ownership, then book him a one-way ticket to Kyrgyzstan. He would never look at the document she'd give him, and he'd never find his way back without her. I don't think he'd know what city he was in if she didn't tell him."

Chris looked at me seriously. "Will she come?"

"I don't know for sure. I think she will at the right price."

"How much?" Chris asked.

"How much can you give her?"

The men looked at each other. Then Jeremy, who I had deduced was the numbers guy, said, "Two hundred K a year, plus a signing bonus."

Kelly nodded. "The signing bonus is key."

"How much for signing?" I asked.

"Fifty thousand."

"That's a big incentive," I said.

"Not if she can run the company," Chris said. Still he looked more concerned than pleased. "You're taking a big risk, you know. If she doesn't come, she'll tell McKay everything. That could seriously hinder our plans."

I nodded slowly. "I know."

We were all quiet for a moment. Then Chris said, "She's really that important?"

I nodded. "Yes."

He thought for a moment, then said, "All right. Do it."

I thought I was an expert at corporate seduction, but I was a neophyte compared to these men. They were financial sirens. Their natural confidence was stunning. I ended up signing the contract before talking to Monica or my lawyer, even before leaving the conference room.

"Where shall I send your executed contracts?" Mila asked.

"I'll take them with me," I said.

"Let me get you something to hold them."

Chris patted me on the back. "Are you ready for the ride of your life, Outlaw James?"

"We'll know soon enough," I replied.

<hr>

That night the five of us ate dinner at Shula's Steak House, a sophisticated restaurant owned by NFL legend Don Shula. At Chris's recommendation I ordered the lobster bisque and the filet mignon and a lobster tail. The food was exquisite. We celebrated my signing with a bottle of Dom Pérignon.

Several times during the meal I caught Mila looking at me. She didn't turn away. Even though I was full, Mila ordered for me the chocolate soufflé for dessert followed by cappuccinos and an expensive scotch. I was surprised at how much alcohol the men could drink. I was feeling tipsy.

Finally, Chris called an end to the evening. "It's been a very good day," he said. "A great start to a promising relationship and venture." He handed Mila his valet ticket. "I need to meet with the guys. Would you mind driving Charles to his hotel?"

"My pleasure," she said. "Your car?"

"Yes," Chris said. "I'll have Kelly drop me off home. Just bring it back in the morning."

⊷⊶⊙⊷⊶

I staggered a little as we walked out to the front of the restaurant. We said good-byes as the valet pulled up in the Bentley. While he held the door for Mila, I climbed into the passenger side, falling back into the luxurious leather seat. My head was foggy.

"Fasten your seat belt, please," Mila said.

"Sorry."

As we pulled away from the restaurant, she asked, "How do you feel?"

"Like I drank too much."

She grinned. "You're not used to these guys' drinking. They drink like sailors."

"I'm not much of a drinker," I said, then added, "Or a sailor."

She laughed. "So outside of drunk, how does it feel to be a twenty-five-year-old millionaire?"

"I'd say I feel . . . validated."

"Validated," she repeated. "I like that. You know, you remind me a lot of Chris."

"How's that?"

"Your ambition. I like ambitious men. Chris gets whatever he wants." She hesitated for a moment, then looked at me. "Do you get what you want, Charles?"

"I try."

"What do you want tonight?"

243

I wasn't sure if she meant what I thought she did. "Sleep," I finally said.

She smiled. "Good answer. Sleep is good."

◆━◉━◆

Mila drove up beneath the hotel's elaborate porte cochere, got out of the car, and gave her keys to the valet. "Please take Mr. James's luggage up to the Presidential Suite."

The young valet was practically falling over her. "Yes, ma'am. Anything else?"

"No," she said, walking away from him. She took my arm and led me into the hotel lobby.

"Did you say *Presidential Suite*?" I asked.

She nodded. "Uh-huh."

Everywhere Mila went people watched. Most were discreet, but not all. One heavy-set bald man just turned and stared at her, following her not only with his eyes but swiveling his head, then his entire body. The woman standing next to him hit him.

"Does that follow you everywhere you go?" I asked.

"Does what follow me?"

"The attention."

She smiled but didn't answer as she walked up to the check-in counter.

"May I help you?" the clerk asked.

"I have the Presidential Suite reserved for Mr. James under the Folger account."

He looked on his computer. "Yes," he said. "Just for the night. How many room keys will you need?"

"Just one; he's alone." Then she turned to me. "Unless you'd like me to spend the night."

I didn't answer. I should have. I should have run.

"It's okay," Mila said playfully, lightly leaning her body into mine. "You're the star tonight. Whatever you want. It will be fun."

I must have looked like a deer in the headlights. Even worse, the alcohol was still making me a little cloudy. That's not an excuse, just the truth. But I didn't say no. Mila turned back to the concierge. "Make it two."

"There you are," he said, handing her the keys. He looked at me with envy.

Mila and I went up to my suite, which was beautifully decorated and roughly the size of most homes in Ogden. My luggage was already inside.

"Let's get you to bed," she said, unbuttoning my shirt.

"I can take it from here," I said. I took off my clothes and climbed into bed. Mila undressed, then turned off the lights and climbed in after me.

In less than twenty-four hours I had betrayed the two most important people in my life.

Chapter Forty

"Wisdom will save you also from the adulterous woman, from the wayward woman with her seductive words. . . . Surely her house leads down to death and her paths to the spirits of the dead." Proverbs 2:16, 18

—CHARLES JAMES'S DIARY

It was still dark the next morning when Mila rolled over, kissed me on the cheek, and got out of bed. She went into the bathroom, then came out dressed and putting on her earrings. "I've arranged a car to pick you up at eleven fifteen," she said softly. "Have a good flight." Then she walked out of the room.

My world felt surreal. *Had that really happened?* I was flooded with guilt. Searing, burning, pressing guilt. I raked my fingers back through my hair. How would I tell Monica? I couldn't tell Monica. Not with how things were. She'd leave me. My head pounded from my hangover. I called room service for coffee and a bag of ice, then lay back in bed. "There is no God but me."

As I lay there my phone rang. I looked over to see who it was. It was Monica. I just looked at it until it stopped ringing. There was no way I could answer. It was no time to talk. I felt transparent. I was too apt to throw myself under the bus.

I was still feeling nauseated as I checked out of the hotel and got in the car. As bad as my hangover was, it was nothing compared to the guilt. I had stepped off a very big cliff and I wanted back on sure ground. But it doesn't work that way. Once you leap, the only choice you have is how you're going to land.

✦━◦✦◦━✦

Sitting at my gate at the Birmingham airport, I called McKay's assistant, Amanda. As usual she answered on the first ring. "Charles. Where are you? McKay's been looking for you."

"I'm at the airport."

"Do you need someone to pick you up?"

"The Birmingham airport."

Pause. "What are you doing there?"

"It's not important," I said. "I need to talk to you. Are you alone?"

"Yes. Why?"

"Are you sure?"

"Of course I'm sure. What's going on?"

I breathed out heavily. I suddenly felt even less sure of how she would respond. I needed to move cautiously. "What I need to ask you is very sensitive."

"If you want to have an affair, you're married," she said flippantly, trying to ease the tension.

The reminder burned. "You know better," I said.

"You sound terrified. What is it?"

"It's risky," I said. "Because once I say what I'm going to say, you're no longer on safe ground. You'll have to make one of the biggest decisions of your life."

She again paused. "Maybe I don't want to hear what you have to say."

"Maybe," I said. "Let me ask you this. How important is money to you?"

"That's certainly direct," she said. "I don't know, how important is eating?"

"So, are you making what you need?"

"That's a very personal question."

"It's a very personal matter."

"All right. Need, yes. *Want* is a different matter. I wouldn't complain if McKay paid me more. Especially since I've given every breath to this company and I see how much they bring in at some of these shows. So yes, I'd like to share a little more in the wealth."

"What is he paying you?"

"Seventy-five. And health and dental. The dental kind of sucks. Where are you going with this, Charles?"

"What if I offered you two hundred thousand a year, with a fifty-thousand-dollar signing bonus?"

There was a long pause. "Doing what?"

"Doing exactly what you're doing now."

She again hesitated. "Is this real?"

"Yes."

"For who?"

"For me."

"And who else?"

"I can't tell you yet."

She was quiet for a moment, then said, "What are you up to?"

"Do I have your attention?"

"Yes."

"More important, do I have your discretion?"

There was another long pause. "You were right," she said. "There is no middle ground. I'm now guilty either way."

"I warned you. Do I have your discretion?"

"Yes."

"Okay. We'll talk tonight if you can get away."

"When do you land?"

"Three forty."

"I'll tell McKay that I'm picking you up. We can talk then. What should I tell him about you being late?"

"Make up something," I said. "It won't be your first time."

"All right. I'll handle it. Just don't let me fall without a net."

Chapter Forty-One

A traitor is always looking for allies.

—CHARLES JAMES'S DIARY

By the time I landed in Des Moines I had two new e-mails. The first was from Chris.

> Charles, we're ready to move. We've set our show in
> Vegas in forty-five days.
> We need to create product ASAP. We need you here.
> We're under the gun. When do you tell McKay you're
> leaving? Can you be back in Birmingham by Friday?

The second e-mail was from Mila.

> Hey, Gorgeous. I ran off so fast I didn't properly thank
> you. I hope I get the chance again soon. Love, Mila
> P.S. You're not just good on stage.

Amanda picked me up at the arrival curb of the Des

Moines airport. She looked nervous. Nervous and guilty. "What have you gotten us into, James?"

"Big money, big lights," I said.

"How did this happen?"

"After the Montgomery show, a man approached me. He's the president of a large investment company with more than a billion dollars in holdings. He offered me my own seminars."

"How much are they paying you?" she asked.

"I'd rather not say."

"I told you mine," she said. "If we're going to cheat together, there can be no secrets."

"A million dollars a year," I said. "Base."

"Whoa," she said. Then added, "You deserve it."

"You're fine with that?"

"Of course. I just want openness between us. So why do they want me?"

"It was my idea. Because you're the most competent person McKay has. You know everything."

"Not everything. I don't know how I'll tell McKay. It will be like a divorce. He'll take it personal."

"Tell him it's not."

She laughed. "Right. So when are you going to tell him?"

"Tomorrow after the show."

"When will you quit?"

"I'm sure he'll quit me immediately, don't you?"

She nodded. "He will. And me. Can you buy me a plane ticket home?"

"No," I said. "But I'll buy you a ticket to Birmingham."

Chapter Forty-Two

I don't know what I was looking for from McKay. Absolution?

—CHARLES JAMES'S DIARY

McKay was already in a foul mood when I went to talk to him. It didn't help that the Des Moines seminar didn't go well. Even though I was again the top money-earner, we brought in about half the usual take, meaning we barely broke even.

McKay had already been drinking for several hours when I got to his room. My announcement only made things worse. Like dropping-an-atom-bomb-on-his-head worse.

"You're quitting," he said, looking at me spitefully. "You're really quitting." It was a statement, not a question.

"Yes."

"Tell me why."

"To pursue other ventures."

His lips pursed. "Other ventures. You're being purposely vague. What are you hiding? What other ventures? Quit hiding behind semantics, you coward. Seminars to compete with mine?"

"Not to compete with yours. But yes. Seminars."

"Finally you're being honest. Stupid, but honest. Unless you're selling tonics and snake oil, you're competing with me." He snorted in anger. "The success has gone to your head, my stupid friend. You have no idea how much time and capital it takes to put something like this together. Millions. And I will bury you."

"I understand."

"And you're still going ahead with it."

"I have investors."

This made him livid. "What did I say when I first met you? Everyone's out for themselves. And you said, 'Not me. I'm different. I could never be your competition.'" He shook his head in disgust. "How many months have you been scheming this?"

"It's not that way. It's been only a few days. Some investors approached me in Montgomery."

"And you jumped for the opportunity before talking to me?"

"They offered me a million dollars."

He took a drink. "You would have made that with me in a few years."

"That's to start. I also get a cut of the show. They're naming the seminars after me."

I saw his face tighten. Then he turned to me with a dark smile. "Congratulations." He looked at me for a moment, then said, "Now tell me this. Are you planning on taking any of my people with you?"

I hesitated. "Amanda."

He threw his glass against the wall, shattering it. "Get out of here!"

"I'm sorry, McKay."

"You will be. I'll see you in court."

Chapter Forty-Three

As anyone who has ever been on a diet can attest, psychologically, once you break down and eat that first cookie, there's little keeping you from finishing off the batch.

—CHARLES JAMES'S DIARY

Amanda and I left Iowa the next morning, flying directly to Birmingham. That evening, I told Monica about the new venture and the million-dollar salary. She wasn't as excited as I had hoped she would be, which made me angry. I thought she was ungrateful. But that was only one way of looking at it. I should have seen that I meant more to her than a million dollars.

"Does this mean I'll see you even less?" she asked.

"For a while," I said.

"All right," she said with a sigh. "Thank you for being honest."

This made my heart ache. I was being anything but honest.

I didn't go home for more than two months. The truth was, it wasn't all because of the new venture. Chris and company would have understood if I had hopped a plane home to see my wife for a weekend. They would have paid for it. It was me. I was afraid to face Monica. I couldn't. She knew me too well. She would know what I'd done.

Part of me reasoned that if it was just a onetime mistake, Monica would forgive me. But I failed that too. Mila didn't leave me alone. I tried to put her off, but she was as persistent as she was beautiful. And she was as masterful at seduction as the men she worked for. Maybe more so. It seemed that the more I pushed back, the more persistent she was. I don't suspect that she had ever had anyone tell her no before. In the end she won and I failed. Miserably.

Businesswise, things came together just as we planned. Better, even. We had product and people. Our first seminar was in Las Vegas. It was a rush seeing my name in eight-foot-high letters in the lobby of the MGM Grand. The last time I had been in Vegas was on the Greyhound bus with Monica. The city had intimidated me then. Now I felt like I was part of it.

The show's profits exceeded everyone's expectations. We brought in more than a million dollars in sales our first day. That night, Chris and his partners threw a wild party in Chris's penthouse suite. I had heard of parties like that but had never been to one. Just about any indulgence you could think of was offered.

During the party Chris took me aside. His face was flushed from drinking. "Our success is only part of the good news."

"There's more?"

"Turns out your previous boss isn't doing too well. Since you left, McKay's last four seminars have lost money. And—twisting the knife—the FTC just filed against him for false claims."

The news didn't make me happy.

"We didn't have anything to do with the FTC, did we?"

"We might have had a little influence," Chris said, raising his glass of vodka to his mouth. "The beauty of it is that even if McKay wins the suit, his company won't survive the investigation."

"There is no God but me," I mumbled.

"What?" Chris asked.

"Nothing."

"You need a drink."

"Yes, I do."

I was getting better at drinking, if you can get better at that. At least I could hold more.

There was a hot tub in the suite, and around three in the morning two women in string bikinis pulled me into the tub and tried to undress me. Mila became furious and stormed off. Dripping wet, I ran down the hall after her. I ended up spending the night with her again.

My world felt completely beyond my control.

The next morning the seminar offices were subdued—almost as if everyone was suffering from a collective hangover. I sent Amanda off to get me a new phone, as mine had been in my pocket when I was pulled into the tub. I spent the morning in Mila's room drinking coffee and sharpening my presentation.

I arrived backstage forty-five minutes before my presentation to speak to the tech people about making some adjustments to lighting. Then I grabbed a can of Coke and sat at the side of the stage watching the running presenter, Bradley Bowen, sell a specialized legal product. Like everyone else in our show, we'd pilfered him from another seminar company.

Just fifteen minutes before I was to go on, I noticed a shadowed female figure approaching me. There was something familiar about the woman's gait and silhouette. Suddenly I realized it was Monica. I stood.

"Monica. What are you doing here?"

Her face was tight and her eyes were puffy. "I came to see if I still had a husband."

"What are you talking about?"

"For four days you haven't returned my calls. Where were you last night?"

"I'm sorry; Chris threw a big celebration party. Things have just been nuts. We brought in more than a million dollars yesterday."

"I don't care," she said. "Why didn't you answer my calls?"

"I don't have a phone," I said emphatically. "It fell in the tub. Amanda just went to get me a new one."

Monica just looked at me, her arms folded at her chest. I went to hug her, but she stepped back.

"I wish you had told me you were coming," I said. "I could have made reservations at one of the Cirque de Soleil shows. We could have celebrated."

"I'm pregnant," she said.

"What?"

"I'm going to have your baby."

For a moment I was speechless. Then I said, "How did this happen?"

"That's a good question. I must have seen you sometime in the last three months. Or maybe I just imagined that and it's an immaculate conception."

My mind spun like one of the casino slot machines. Just then the stage manager shouted, "You have ten minutes, Charles."

"Got it," I shouted to him. I turned back to Monica. Her eyes had welled up and she looked pale, as if she were about to faint.

She wiped her eyes, then asked, "Do you have something to tell me?" She was looking at me with an intensity I'd never seen before.

"What are you talking about?"

There was an angry but desperate look in her eyes. "Charles, I'm giving you a chance. Do you have something to tell me?"

I feigned a smile. "Monica, I don't know what you're getting at. Really."

She looked down for a moment and put her hand over her eyes and started to cry.

I reached out to comfort her. "Honey . . ."

"Don't touch me!" she screamed. When she looked back up, her eyes were wet but hard. "Who is Mila?"

My chest froze. And my mouth. I couldn't speak.

"McKay sent me the e-mails from your account. Who is she? Other than your new love."

It took me a long time to answer. "She's no one important."

Monica's voice came out angry and broken. "Apparently she's more important than me." She took off her wedding ring and set it on a stool. "I'm not your pearl."

That was the last time I saw Monica.

Chapter Forty-Four

In my quest to have it all, I have lost it all.

—CHARLES JAMES'S DIARY

Dr. Fordham sat back in her chair. "How long ago was that?"

"About eight years."

"Did she have the baby?"

"A boy. Gabriel."

"Have you seen him?"

"Not in person. I've seen pictures."

"Why didn't you go back to her?"

"Pride. I kept waiting for her to reach out."

"How long did you wait?"

"A few months. Until the tour ended."

"And when she didn't come back?"

"I was angry. I couldn't believe that after all I'd given her she could just leave me like that."

Dr. Fordham cocked her head to one side. "All you'd given her?"

"The money, the car, the home in Santa Monica . . ."

"A baby?"

I looked at her.

"She needed you, not things. Especially once she became pregnant."

I took a deep breath. "I know."

"What happened then?"

"I felt desperate. I called and texted her at least fifty times, but she wouldn't answer. After that I think I went into a depression for a while. Maybe I'm still in one. That's where we are now."

"Do you realize that what you just described are the stages of grief?"

"What do you mean?"

"A psychiatrist named Elisabeth Kübler-Ross described a series of emotional stages that people go through when confronting a death. They're basically what you described: denial, anger, bargaining, depression, and finally acceptance. The only thing I haven't heard yet is acceptance."

"Maybe because she's not dead," I said tersely.

"Someone doesn't have to be dead for you to mourn them."

I shifted uncomfortably on the couch.

"Have you ever thought of just going back and talking to her in person?"

"Many times."

"Why didn't you?"

I lowered my head. "Shame. It's been eight years. You can't go back to how things were. Nothing stays the same."

"You're right," she said. "Nothing stays the same. Everything changes. But sometimes for the better."

"I don't think she'd take me back."

"But you don't know that." She shifted in her seat. "Let me ask you something. If Monica called right now and asked you to come back, would you?"

I looked down for a moment, and then the words spilled out almost as if by their own will. "Yes. I would."

Dr. Fordham paused to let the epiphany settle in my mind. "You know better than anyone that some things are worth fighting for. You've spent your whole life fighting. You're a fighter."

I let out a deep breath. The conversation had exceeded my pain tolerance. I raked my hair back with my hand. "I don't know."

"I know it's a lot," she said. "It's okay to think about it."

I nodded slowly, then I looked up at the clock on the wall. It was three minutes to the hour. "We're out of time but can I ask you one more thing? If you have time. You said you're meeting a friend."

"I'm okay," she said. "Go ahead."

"I had the dream again last night. Only it was worse."

"How was it worse?"

"It was more real. There was more fire. There were sirens."

"What kind of sirens?"

"Emergency vehicles. There were dozens of them like there had been some kind of catastrophic accident." I took a deep breath. "I want to ask you something. It's a little out there . . ."

She looked at me intently. "Yes?"

"Do you believe that dreams can be prophetic?"

She hesitated before answering. "If you're asking if I think you'll find yourself walking Route 66 surrounded by flames, no, I don't."

"I meant in general."

"I usually don't comment on psychic phenomena—not because I don't believe that it exists, but because I don't have any means to prove that it does or to understand it. Having said that, I don't rule out the possibility that, in some cases, prophetic dreams and intuition could exist. There are certainly historic precedents. If you believe the Bible—"

"I don't," I said quickly.

"Even if you take the Bible as an archetype, it's still an indication of humanity's belief in prophetic dreams, like Daniel and King Nebuchadnezzar's dream of a stone cut without hands, or Joseph interpreting Pharaoh's dream about Egypt's future famine."

Of course I was familiar with both stories.

"There are recorded instances of prophetic dreams in secular history as well. Abraham Lincoln had a dream that he walked into the Oval Office to find a wake in progress. When he asked a soldier who had died, he was told that the president had been killed by an assassin. Ten days later Lincoln was assassinated in Ford's Theatre."

"That's what I was afraid of," I said. "This dream of mine . . . it seems to be headed somewhere."

She looked at me thoughtfully. "I've been thinking a lot about your dream. I've had an interesting idea. Would you consider walking part of the route?"

"What part?"

"It doesn't really matter except that it looks like what you're seeing in your dream. Just walk it. See what happens. It might help release your mind from whatever it's stuck on. Ultimately, what you're experiencing is fear. And usually the best way to remove the fear of something is to confront it head on. I think to actually walk the road might bring you relief."

"And if it doesn't?"

She grinned. "Then you've had a nice walk. It certainly won't hurt you. I think that if everyone walked an hour a day, half the mental illness in this country would disappear."

I considered her request. "I can do that," I said. "I was already planning on driving it."

She looked at me with surprise. "You were?"

"A few months ago I planned a trip on Route 66 with a few friends. We're going to drive the route on Harleys."

Her look of surprise deepened. "You didn't tell me that. Was that before or after your dreams started?"

I had to think about it. "I think it was a few days after."

"Do you think your dreams might have something to do with the trip?"

"I have no idea." I took a deep breath and exhaled slowly. Too much to think about. "I better let you get on with your Saturday. Thank you for coming in."

"You're welcome. Good luck on your tour."

"Thank you. I'm going to need it."

"How long will you be gone?"

"About six weeks."

"Would you like to schedule an appointment for when you get back?"

"Yes, but I better wait a few weeks to see how things are going. Sometimes we end up extending these things."

She walked me to the office's outer door. "Go ahead. I need to lock up in here."

"Thanks again. I'll see you in a few weeks."

She smiled at me. "Good luck on your journey," she said.

Later, I wondered why she had used the word *journey*. She was so in tune. It made me wonder if, on some level, she knew what was to come.

Chapter Forty-Five

My life is spent in details.

—CHARLES JAMES'S DIARY

MONDAY, MAY 2

There were a million details I needed to tend to before I left on tour. Both at home and at work. The conference center in Boston had scheduled the wrong room, reserving a hall for us that could accommodate only seventy-five people. They had already booked the grand ballroom for another event, forcing us to either cancel or scramble to find a new venue. Fortunately, the Boston advertising hadn't started yet.

Amanda, Glenn, and I ate lunch in the conference room while we went line by line down each event to ensure that we had the right location and the right marketing, personnel, and product. Six weeks, forty-two days, twenty-one cities, round and round we go. There's a reason they call it a whirlwind tour.

We finished our meeting after seven thirty. Amanda and Glenn invited me to join them for dinner but I still had too much to do before leaving. I had been inside for so long that I hadn't even noticed that it had been raining, though it was only a light mist as I walked out to the parking garage.

I drove home and packed. My phone kept ringing with last-minute questions, many of which had no urgency. *I'm going on a sales tour, not dying*, I thought. After the fifth call I shut off my phone.

I left a mess for my cleaners. I wrote them a note reminding them to reset the home alarm after they left.

I didn't get everything done I wanted to, but worse case, I had Amanda. She wasn't joining me until the end of the second week. She had a key to my house and the code to my alarm. Anything I missed she could take care of.

Around midnight I turned my phone back on so I'd be notified if there was a change in flights. I was too keyed up to sleep, so I went to my home theater and began channel surfing. I ended up watching an old musical called *Finian's Rainbow* before dragging myself to bed at around three in the morning.

The truth was, as much as I needed it, I was afraid to go to sleep. To sleep, perchance to dream. I was terrified of having the dream.

Chapter Forty-Six

It begins.

—CHARLES JAMES'S DIARY

TUESDAY, MAY 3

I had the dream again. It was the most horrific version yet. And the most lucid. The sirens and screaming were so loud that I knelt on the broken road and covered my ears. That's how I was positioned when I woke, crouched into a ball with my hands over my ears. For the first time I woke myself screaming.

After meeting with Dr. Fordham I had looked up the story of Abraham Lincoln dreaming of his own death. Those close to the president said that after the dream he was deeply troubled—all the way up to his assassination less than two weeks later. That's exactly how I felt. Deeply troubled. I still had no idea what I was supposed to do with it. But I couldn't imagine it getting any worse.

I looked over at the clock. It was nine thirty. It was

dark for so late in the morning. I got up and looked out the window. The sky was overcast. The street in front of my house was wet but it wasn't raining. I went for my phone but it wasn't in my room. I'd left it in front of the television.

As I walked downstairs, the sound of thunder reverberated through the house. I hated flying on days like this. I poured myself a glass of apple juice and went to the theater. My phone was on the floor. I'd forgotten to charge it. I picked it up and turned it on. The battery life was down to 7 percent. There was a text from Amanda.

Call me when you can

I checked the phone and saw that I had missed several of her calls. I pressed her entry in my contacts. Amanda answered on the first ring. "You turned your phone off again?"

"I left it in the other room."

"Do you still want me to drive you to the airport?"

"Yes."

"Are you coming in before you go?"

"I wasn't planning on it."

"If you have time, it would be good for you to talk to the troops before you leave. It always gets them fired up." When I didn't answer, she said, "Please."

I really didn't want to, but Amanda rarely made requests, and I hated to deny them when she did. "All right. Give me an hour. I'm not dressed yet."

Amanda pulled into my driveway at a quarter past eleven. Her white BMW was beaded with water. I lugged my largest suitcase out the front door as she came up my walkway.

"Sorry I'm late," she said. "I got caught in a downpour just outside the city. Can I help you with something?"

"I still need to get my backpack and lock up. You can drag this behemoth to your car. If you can."

She looked at the bag. "Yikes. You usually pack light. Why are you taking such a big suitcase?"

"I'm carrying sales contracts," I said. "They almost ran out in Toledo and don't have enough for Cincinnati."

"That's a good thing," she said.

"Yes, that's a good thing."

I went into the house and got my backpack, then set the alarm and walked out, locking the dead bolt. Amanda was standing behind the suitcase near the open trunk of her car.

"I can't lift it," she said.

"I'll get it." As I walked to the car, I said, "By the way, I've set the alarm. Just in case you need to get in."

"Only if I have to."

"You probably will," I said. "I probably left something on."

⊶═◉═⊷

It started raining again as we drove downtown. Amanda asked, "How are you feeling about things?"

"Optimistic," I said. "It's our biggest tour ever. We've got our best product."

"I think this will be our best year ever. What's the goal?"

"Fifty-seven million."

"You might be able to live off that."

"If I wasn't paying so many people," I said.

"Maybe you should try going on tour without so many people," she replied.

"You've gotten snarky," I said.

She grinned. "I've learned from the best."

We hit the early lunch traffic, and with the rain, it took us nearly an hour to make the office. As we went up in the elevator, Amanda said, "The troops are assembled in the conference room."

"All right. I need to hit my office. I'll see you there."

I went into my office and plugged my phone into the wall to charge it, then walked out to the conference room. I could see people through the frosted glass but they weren't moving. The door was shut. Something was up. I reached down and opened the door.

"Surprise!" My staff broke into a chorus of "Happy Birthday."

When they finished, I said, "The surprise is it's not my birthday."

"I know," Amanda said. "But you'll be on the road when it is, and we wanted to celebrate with you."

"You think of everything."

"It's my job."

There was a large double-chocolate fudge cake with chocolate buttercream frosting and brown-butter almond brittle ice cream from Jeni's Splendid Ice Creams.

"That's my favorite ice cream," I said.

"I know," Amanda said.

I got some cake and ice cream, then stayed in the room just long enough to eat and thank everyone. By the time I finished, it was time to leave for the airport. I said good-bye and went to my office. I logged out of my computer and unplugged my phone. It now had only 2 percent battery life. "Amanda."

She walked into my office. "Yes?"

"I've had my phone plugged in for the last hour, but it didn't charge."

"Which outlet did you use?"

"Why does that matter?"

"Something's wrong with the outlets along the south wall. I already called the landlord. Maintenance is coming tomorrow to fix them."

"That would have been good information to have an hour ago."

"I'm sorry. We can charge it on the way to the airport. We need to leave. It's raining buckets out there."

I slipped my phone into my coat pocket. "What airline am I flying out on?"

"United," she said. Before I could ask she said, "Delta didn't have any first-class seats available. Will you drive?"

As I signaled to pull out of the parking garage, I handed Amanda my cell phone. "Will you charge that?"

"Of course. Where's your charger?"

I glanced over at her. "In my car. You don't have one?"

"I don't have the same phone as you. I have a Samsung."

I groaned. "Who needs a phone?"

About fifteen minutes later Amanda's phone beeped indicating a text message. "Your flight's delayed a little."

"How little?"

"Twelve minutes."

"That's good. I won't have to trample people in the security line."

The drive to O'Hare from downtown Chicago is about eighteen miles, but with the rain and traffic it took us almost an hour, eliminating the extra time I thought I'd have. I pulled Amanda's car up to the curb outside the departures door of the United terminal.

"I want you to change my hotel from the Cincinnatian to the Millennium."

"You love the Cincinnatian. It's a classic hotel."

"The last time I was there it took me a half hour to check in. Make sure I'm on the concierge level. I think it's the seventh floor."

"It's the eleventh floor. And this time of the year they're probably sold-out. But I know the manager. I'll see what I can do. If they don't have a suitable room, do you still want to stay at the Cincinnatian?"

"Fine, just don't forget to text me. I don't want to get there and not know where I'm going."

"Your phone's dead, remember?"

I shook my head. "Right. I'll try to charge it before I fly. Does my plane have power outlets?"

"I'm sorry, I don't know. Do you want me to check?"

"No, if I can't charge it, I'll call you from a pay phone. If you see a number you don't recognize—"

"I'll look for the Cincinnati area code."

As I reached for the door latch she said, "Wait, I have some cash for you." She dug into her purse and brought out a bank envelope. "There's three thousand."

"Why so much?"

"The temp company we employed in Indiana wants to be paid in cash. It's around seventeen hundred. And I put in a little extra for you. For tips and such."

"Thank you." I grabbed my backpack from the backseat and put the envelope in it. Then I pushed the button on the console that opened the trunk, and I got out of the car. Amanda likewise got out and walked around to the back of her car as I pulled the bag out.

"That thing's going to give you a hernia," she said. "Just don't collect anything. Have a good show. I'll meet you in a couple of weeks."

"Thanks." I slammed shut the trunk and we briefly embraced. She actually looked sad that I was leaving. "Keep the home fires burning," I said.

"I always do. Have a good tour. Knock 'em dead."

"I always do," I replied. "I'll see you in a couple of weeks."

Amanda got back in her car. I waved to her as she pulled away from the curb, merging back into the flow of traffic like a fish thrown back into a river.

I suddenly felt alone. I took a deep breath. "There is no God but me."

Chapter Forty-Seven

In spite of my best efforts to the contrary, someone saved my life today.

—CHARLES JAMES'S DIARY

The airport was crowded, even by O'Hare standards. Lightning had delayed a few flights and the typical domino effect was in play, changing flight times and turning people into raving lunatics as they missed their connections.

Fortunately, my flight from Chicago to Cincinnati was nonstop and just a little more than an hour long. I checked my bag at the ticket counter and got a paper boarding pass. I usually used my phone to check in but it was now completely dead.

The security line seemed to move in slow motion. To further add to my delay, TSA randomly pulled my bag off the conveyor and ran it through one of their bomb-sniffing machines before returning it to me. By the time I got to my gate there was already a large crowd gathered in the corridor while passengers from the incoming flight emerged from the Jetway.

The gate agent, an older woman with dyed black hair, made an announcement. "For those waiting for Flight 227 to Cincinnati, we are still hoping for as close to an on-time departure as possible. Once we have finished disembarking our incoming passengers, we will begin boarding immediately. We will begin with parents traveling with infants and those needing extra assistance boarding. Please have your tickets ready."

I considered walking up to the priority lane to wait but decided instead to pick up a charger for my phone. There was a gift shop just two gates down the terminal.

I found a portable charger for my phone and then, figuring I had plenty of time for the mob to board, I perused the magazines. I ended up with a copy of the *Robb Report*, *USA Today*, a couple of energy shots, and a bag of gummy candy.

There was a long line in the store and just one open cash register. When I got back to my gate I was surprised to find the line gone. I guess they really were serious about that on-time departure. The gate agent, who still had a line at her counter, lifted a microphone to her mouth.

"This is the final boarding call for Flight 227 to Cincinnati. All passengers should be boarded at this time. Mr. Yin Cheng and Mr. Charles James, please report immediately to the check-in gate. Your flight has boarded and we will be closing the boarding door. Mr. Yin Cheng and Mr. Charles James, please report immediately to the check-in gate."

"I'm here," I said, raising my hand.

She left the counter, walking over to the podium. "Are you Mr. Cheng or Mr. James?"

"Did you really ask that?" I said, handing her my ticket.

She didn't smile. On a flight day like today, she was past snide. "There you go, Mr. James. Thank you for your Premier status. Have a good flight."

"Thank you."

I walked down the Jetway. There were at least a dozen passengers near the end of the corridor waiting to board and a crewman was still gathering the carry-on baggage that people had left outside the plane's entrance. That's when I realized I didn't have my backpack. I figured that I must have left it back at the gift shop. With my computer and the large amount of cash in it, if it wasn't already stolen, it soon would be. I turned around and ran back down the Jetway.

The boarding door was still open, and as I walked out of the Jetway, the gate agent was back at the counter helping a disgruntled customer.

I unsuccessfully tried to get her attention, then decided it would be faster to just retrieve my pack. As I ran to the store I watched the people emerging from it to see if anyone had my pack. No one did.

I frantically walked around the store but couldn't find my pack. There were four people in line with only one employee at the counter—a different woman from the one who had just helped me. I walked ahead of the line to the other side of the cash register.

"Excuse me, miss, but my flight's literally leaving in two minutes. Did someone turn in a backpack?"

The female clerk slowly glanced up at me. "I don't know. I just got here." She went back to scanning another customer's purchases.

"I'm sorry to inconvenience you," I said tersely, "but there was a lot of money in that bag, *and* my laptop. They're about to close the door on my flight. Could you please take just ten seconds to check and see if someone turned it in?"

She looked at me with indifference. "I'm busy."

"Oh, come on," I said.

The woman she was helping looked at me sympathetically. "It's okay. I can wait."

The clerk sighed, then walked out from the counter and through a door to a back room. I assumed she'd be right back, but she wasn't. After a full minute I was about to knock on the door when she suddenly emerged holding my pack. "Is this it?"

"Yes," I said, grabbing it from her. "Thank you." I swung the pack over one shoulder and ran back to my gate. When I got there the boarding door was closed. The agent was still at the counter surrounded by even more people. I walked up to the door and tried to open it myself, but it was locked.

"Sir, what are you doing?" the agent asked.

I turned to her. "That's my flight."

"The aircraft door is closed." She looked at me with a peculiar expression. "Didn't I just check you in?"

"I had to get my pack. Could you please open the door?"

"I'm sorry, once the door is closed, I can't reopen it."

"But the plane hasn't left yet. I can see it," I said, gesturing to the plane. "It's right there."

"I'm sorry, sir. There are regulations. You never should have left the flight."

"I didn't have a choice," I said, doing my best to remain calm. "Come on. It will take you two seconds."

"I'm really sorry sir," she said. She didn't sound sorry at all.

"What am I supposed to do now?"

"There's a scheduling desk three gates down. They can help you."

"I'll give you a hundred dollars to open the door."

She looked at me incredulously. "You're trying to bribe me?"

"What are you, a cop? Yes, I am. Two hundred dollars."

"Sir, I don't have the authority. I suggest you go directly to the customer service desk."

I couldn't believe I was going to miss a flight that was still right in front of me. The agent turned back to the other customers she was helping.

I hiked angrily down to the customer service center. Not surprisingly, the place was as crowded as a Walmart on Black Friday. There were only four agents and each of them had a long line.

I stood in what turned out to be the slowest of the lines for nearly a half hour, growing increasingly impatient. Actually, impatience seemed to be the order of the day. One red-faced man was cursing and yelling threats at the agent until he was forcibly removed by police.

This is a madhouse, I thought. Then, with just one person in front of me, sirens suddenly blared throughout the airport. Not a minute later, all the flights on every screen registered DELAYED or DIVERTED.

The agent in front of me said, "Oh dear God . . ."

Somewhere from the corridor a woman screamed.

"What's going on?" I asked.

The agent looked pale. "A plane has crashed."

"Which one?"

He looked down at his screen. "United flight 227. Cincinnati."

Chapter Forty-Eight

The nightmare is real. It's all real.

—CHARLES JAMES'S DIARY

United Flight 227, the flight I was ticketed on, had crashed shortly after takeoff. At the time, that's all I knew. It's all anyone knew.

The atmosphere around the airport was indescribable as stranded travelers roamed aimlessly in a surreal state of disbelief and shock. They talked in whispers or nervously loud voices. Some were crying. Some wailed. A group of people were crouched down around a woman who had fainted.

It was only minutes before the airport television monitors started showing pictures of the crash. Some people flocked to the television screens, while others gathered at the east windows and looked out toward the billowing column of smoke.

Then came a frightening cacophony of sirens. It sounded like there were hundreds of them wailing and chirping, the sound as thick as the smoke from the crash.

Suddenly it occurred to me that this was my dream—my nightmare come true. It was all here: the people wailing, the sirens, the fire. And there was fear. Palpable fear and the unknown that precipitated it. What had happened? Had someone done this? Was there more to come?

The chaos wreaked havoc on my OCD. I had to get out of the airport. As I made my way to the exit, police, some with leashed dogs, ran past me into the terminal. I stumbled out of the airport and to the taxi stand. The sidewalks were oddly bare. I couldn't understand why everyone wasn't leaving. Or maybe I did. It felt like I was leaving the scene of an accident.

I walked up to a waiting taxi, opened the back door, threw my pack across the vinyl seat, and climbed in after it. The taxi driver, a young Jamaican man, said, "Where are you going, boss?"

"Downtown," I said. "Michigan Boulevard Building."

"Yes, boss. Right away."

He pulled away from the curb as a black SWAT van pulled in behind us. As he drove off I thought, *Why am I going to my office? What am I going to do there?* The only person I really wanted to see right then was Dr. Fordham. Or a bartender. *That's what I need. A strong drink. Maybe a dozen of them.*

"Change of plans," I said. "Take me to the Green Door Tavern. Over on Orleans."

"No problem, boss."

As we drove from the terminal enclosure a massive plume of smoke was visible to the east. There was subdued chatting coming from the taxi's radio, and the driver reached down and turned it up. It was a news report about the crash.

"Could you turn that down, please?" I said.

"Yes, boss." He glanced at me in the rearview mirror. "You know there was a plane crash."

"I know."

"There were no survivors."

"How do you know that?"

"They say it on the radio."

I was silent for nearly a minute before I said, "There was *one*."

He again glanced at me in his rearview mirror but said nothing. Neither of us spoke again until we reached the bar.

Chapter Forty-Nine

God or Fate has pressed the cosmic reset button of my life.

—CHARLES JAMES'S DIARY

The Green Door Tavern has been a popular Chicago watering hole since 1872. It was a speakeasy during Prohibition, procuring its liquor from no less than Al Capone. The interior is lushly decorated with antique Americana, an eclectic collage of neon, old carnival posters, Tiffany glass, and commercial signage from the early twentieth century, some authentic, some made in China.

I was glad to see that the patronage was light with just a few tables occupied. I set my pack on the parquet floor beneath the bar and sat down on a stool a few yards from a man in a suit who greeted me with a slight nod. He was holding a nearly empty mug of beer and his face was slightly flushed from inebriation.

The bartender walked up to me. "What can I get you?"

"G and T," I said. "A double. To start."

"That'll be right up."

On the television screen behind the bar there was video of a burning airplane above the banner "Breaking News: Flight 227, Plane Crash at O'Hare."

The man next to me was staring at the screen. He turned to me and said in a hoarse voice, "And you thought you were having a bad day."

"I thought I was," I said. I turned back toward the television as the bartender set my drink on the counter in front of me. "There you are. One G and T double."

"Thank you."

"Let me know if you need anything else."

I took a drink. After a minute, I said to the businessman, "I was supposed to be on that flight."

"That one?" he said, pointing at the television. "That burning chunk of metal?"

"Flight 227 to Cincinnati." I reached into my inner coat pocket and brought out my ticket stub. "Look at this."

I handed him the stub. He examined it and handed it back. "You're not joking. You missed your flight?"

"It was closer than that," I said, returning the ticket to my back pocket. "I actually checked in. I was about to board when I realized that I'd left my backpack in one of the shops, and I ran to get it. When I got back they had already closed the doors. The gate agent wouldn't let me on."

"You owe that gate agent a drink," he said. "At least." He took a sip. "You're saying that you checked in to the flight?"

"Yes."

He suddenly started laughing.

"Why is that so funny?"

"You're telling me that you actually checked in."

"Yes. I did."

"And the agent ran your ticket through the machine."

"Of course."

"Did the gate agent ever take your name off the flight list?"

"No. She was busy." I suddenly realized what he was driving at. "They think I was on that flight."

"So everyone thinks you're dead."

"They will."

He slapped the counter. "You are the luckiest man on the planet. I've fantasized about what I'd do if something like that ever happened to me. One minute you've got the world on your shoulders, the next, poof, you're off the grid. No taxes, no responsibilities, nothing. You're invisible. You're the invisible man, untouchable as a ghost." He slowly shook his head. "Man, oh man, what I would give to be you right now." His voice lowered. "You, my friend, are free. You can start a whole new life."

I looked at him for a moment. "It's like pushing a reset button."

He laughed. "That's exactly what it is." He raised his glass again. "To the cosmic reset button." He downed the rest of his beer, then banged his empty glass onto the counter with a loud clang. The bartender glanced over at us.

"Another pilsner, please." He turned back to me. "So now what are you going to do?"

"I don't know."

"I know what I'd do. Nothing. I'd contact no one. Not a soul. Then, while everyone is in mourning, I'd drain all the money from my bank accounts before they're frozen, and then I'd figure out what I really wanted from life."

"You really have thought this through."

"I told you I had," he said. "You could do anything. You could kill someone, and they'd never come looking for you." He smiled as if he were suddenly lost in his fantasy. "I'd definitely attend my own funeral. That would be a must. But you'd have to be in disguise—fake beard, glasses." He shook his head. "No, screw that. Too risky. Someone might recognize you. You have family? A wife?"

"No."

"That's going to make it easier. It's going to take some time to figure out what you want, but what do you care? You got all the time in the world. At least until someone recognizes you. Then it's over." The bartender set another beer in front of the man. He turned to me. "What are you drinking?"

"Gin and tonic."

"A gin and tonic for my dead friend."

The bartender glanced over at me, and I shrugged. As he prepared my drink, the man said, "When you sat down, I thought you looked a little familiar. I was going to ask your name, but I won't. You've got to protect that. You've got one shot at this. Don't waste it. Get out of town. Go someplace they don't recognize you, to an island or something. Go for a long walk."

Chapter Fifty

I can think of no reason that my life was spared. Not one.

—CHARLES JAMES'S DIARY

The man left about ten minutes after our conversation, but not without giving me his business card. He was an attorney at a well-known downtown law firm in a building just two blocks from mine.

"Call me after you resurface," he said. "If you ever do. I want to know how this turns out."

I took his card. Still reeling, I ate dinner at the bar—their signature Bootlegger burger, with bacon, an over-easy egg, and whiskey ketchup.

As I ate, I watched continuing news coverage of the crash. Someone had captured video of the crash on their cell phone, which the station played and replayed continually. When they weren't showing pictures of the plane crashing or firemen trying to douse the burning fuselage, there were talking heads conjecturing about what had gone wrong.

New information continued to trickle in. The doomed plane was a Boeing 757-200. It carried 13 crew and 199 passengers.

According to reports, all 212 passengers and crew members were killed on impact. Of course, there was no way they could have really known that. I hope they were all killed on impact. Being burned alive was something I didn't want to think about.

Initially, some had suspected terrorism, a charge that was later discredited by the authorities, who hinted at pilot error. It would be weeks before FAA investigators determined that the crash was caused by mechanical malfunction. As the jet was beginning to take off, one of the engines separated from its mounts, damaging the wing and severing the hydraulic lines that kept the wing locked in place. As the jet started to climb, the left wing stalled while the right wing continued to lift, rolling the jet sideways and causing it to crash.

The plane had just been refueled, so by the time emergency personnel doused the flames, there was nothing left but a charred fuselage. Nothing could have survived the heat of the inferno. One commentator stated that it was doubtful that any human remains would even be found. "Jet fuel, in open air," he said, "can burn as hot as a crematorium." What that meant was there were not only no survivors, there were no traces of the dead either.

That included me. For all intents and purposes I, like them, no longer existed. What do you do when the world thinks you're dead, when you no longer exist? Maybe my bar mate was right. Whatever you want.

Chapter Fifty-One

I am a ghost.

—CHARLES JAMES'S DIARY

I didn't leave the pub until after dark. I caught a cab outside the bar and had the driver take me to a thrift shop, where I bought some cheap sweatpants, a hoodie, a pair of Converse tennis shoes, and a pair of sunglasses.

I changed inside the store, carrying my suit out in one of their sacks. I remembered that my name was embroidered inside my suit coat. I ripped out the panel of fabric that had my name on it and tossed the suit in the Dumpster outside the store. A peculiar thought crossed my mind. How thrilled I would have been, as a kid, to have found that coat.

It was after ten when the cab reached my neighborhood.

"Which house?" the driver asked.

"Just pull over there," I said, pointing to the curb near the back of my house. I didn't want him pulling into my driveway and attracting attention.

He rolled up to the curb. I handed him his fare in cash and grabbed my pack. I looked around to make sure that no one was around or looking out their windows. Then I got out. The taxi sped away.

I dropped my pack over the fence and climbed over. I unlocked my back door from a keypad and went in, disarming the alarm system. I knew that this action could be traced by the alarm company but there was no reason they would even look. I was dead. A corpse. A lapsed subscription. End of story.

I turned on only a few inner lights. I got a beer out of my refrigerator, then went up to my bedroom and turned on the television to watch more news.

The plane crash was the lead story nationally as well as locally. The shutting down of O'Hare had wreaked havoc on the entire airline industry, resulting in the cancellation of more than a thousand flights from coast to coast. The questions kept coming, spinning in my mind like a roulette wheel.

What if I hadn't forgotten to charge my phone? What if the wall outlets had been working? Then I wouldn't have gone to buy a charger. Or what if the line in the store had been shorter? What if I hadn't stopped at all?

At the root of all these questions was a bigger question. *Why was my life spared when so many others weren't? Was it just a coincidence? If not, why would the universe pick a sinner like me?*

I couldn't come to any conclusion. None of it made sense. The beer didn't help. A little after midnight I drank another and fell asleep on the couch.

Chapter Fifty-Two

I'm going to finish my dream. I'm going to walk.

—CHARLES JAMES'S DIARY

I woke the next morning with my head pounding and the sun in my eyes. I looked out the window. The storm was gone. That was something. And I hadn't had the dream. Actually, I had lived it. Maybe it was finally over. Or then again, maybe everything was just beginning.

I rolled over and looked at my clock. It was ten past nine. My company's workday had started. Those who didn't already know of my demise were finding out about now. I could imagine the insanity of that. Or maybe not. Truthfully, I had no idea how they would respond. They would be upset, no doubt, if not for me, then because their jobs had died in the crash.

Amanda would have been the first to know. She always tracked my flights, so she probably knew within minutes of the crash. She was the only one at work that I really worried about. I didn't doubt that she would mourn me.

If there were to be a funeral, Amanda would be the one to arrange it. I couldn't help but wonder if there would be a funeral or if the lack of a corpse would change that. Maybe there'd just be a memorial service. Or maybe they'd just go out for a drink and call it good.

More questions. I wondered if my mother or brother would ever find out and what they'd do when they did. Or was I already dead and buried to them?

Most of all, what would Monica think? Would she mourn me? Or had she already mourned me enough? Would she even care?

The biggest question of all still remained: What was I going to do now?

McKay's words echoed back to me: *The more I unplug from the matrix, the more I find myself. Walk away. Walk as far and as fast as you can.* And then there was the man in the bar. *You've got one shot at this. Don't waste it. Get out of town. Go someplace they don't recognize you, to an island or something. Go for a long walk.*

It seemed that the universe kept hinting at walking. Even in my recurring dream. Of course, the obvious thing to do was to just go back to my life. At that moment I confronted the raw truth: I didn't *want* to go back to my life. I wasn't happy. I kept myself insanely busy just to avoid the quiet moments of loneliness and regret. In many ways I was as miserable as I had been as a child. The only real happiness I remembered had been those few years of bliss with Monica. What had I traded her love for?

In my first session with Dr. Fordham, she had questioned my dream. Why would the route start where I was and end where Monica was? At the time I told her that it was of no consequence, but even then, subliminally, I must have known she was right. That's why I got so upset when she suggested it. The fact that I was walking Route 66 to Monica was no more a coincidence than the fire and wailing and sirens of a plane crash. My subconscious and Dr. Fordham had shown me what I was afraid to admit—if Monica would take me back, I would go to her, leaving all else behind. I would sell all I had to purchase the one pearl of great price.

At that moment I knew what I was going to do. What I had to do. Maybe I'd known all along. I was going to walk. Just as my dream, McKay, Dr. Fordham, and some stranger in a bar had said I should. I would walk as far away from my broken life as I could. It was only fitting that I would travel back on a broken road.

And I would walk to *her*. And in my journey I would show her that I had changed and that I was willing to take a chance that she might forgive me. For whatever reason, fate, the universe, or just stupid dumb luck had given me a second chance at life. Maybe Monica would do the same.

Acknowledgments

This book is a year late. Thankfully. The book I would have written, had I turned it in on time, would have been filled with anger and anguish. I would like to thank my friend Jonathan Karp, editor Trish Todd, Carolyn Reidy, and the Simon & Schuster family who stuck by me during a very difficult personal time. Without your kindness, love, and support, this book never would have been possible. Thank you to my new editor, Christine Pride. You hit the ground running! This book is much better because of your input and insight. I look forward to our future together. Also, thank you to my agent, Laurie Liss, who was and is always there for me and my family.

The Broken Road is loosely based on a real life, a true story of redemption. The first time I met the very successful man who inspired my main character, Charles

James, he humbly told me that he was a sinner, but was hoping God would someday forgive him. The horrific childhood I describe in this book contains much of his truth. Way too much. For this reason, he has asked to remain anonymous so as to not bring pain to anyone. So here I thank my anonymous friend for inspiring me with a story of redemption. I believe that God has already forgiven you.

Coming Soon

The
Forgotten
Road

The journey continues Spring 2018